Buckskin Bandit

★★★★★

Winnie

The Horse Gentler

8

Tyndale House Publishers, Inc.
Carol Stream, Illinois

·* Buckskin Bandit *·

DANDI DALEY MACKALL

Visit Tyndale's exciting Web site for kids at www.tyndale.com/kids and the
Winnie the Horse Gentler Web site at www.winniethehorsegentler.com.

You can contact Dandi Daley Mackall through her Web site at
www.dandibooks.com.

TYNDALE is a registered trademark of Tyndale House Publishers, Inc.

The Tyndale Kids logo is a trademark of Tyndale House Publishers, Inc.

Buckskin Bandit

Designed by Jacqueline L. Nuñez

Edited by Ramona Cramer Tucker

Scripture quotations are taken from the *Holy Bible,* New Living Translation,
copyright © 1996 by Tyndale House Foundation. Used by permission
of Tyndale House Publishers, Inc., Carol Stream, Illinois 60188. All rights
reserved.

For manufacturing information regarding this product, please call
1-800-323-9400.

ISBN 978-0-8423-8724-8, mass paper

Printed in the United States of America

16   15   14
10   9   8   7   6

For Ramona Cramer Tucker,
my amazing and talented editor,
who helps me keep "Winnie's world" straight.
Thanks for your friendship.
And thanks to Jeff and Kayla for sharing you.

Dear Winnie the Horse Gentler,
    I know you're terrific with horses. But how R U with parents?? I LOVE my Paint, but my parents are driving me crazy! Whenever I go 2 a horse show, they HAVE 2 come along. Then they worm their way to the arena and clap and cheer every time I go around. And if I win, they scream so loud! It's totally embarrassing! Can you help?
—Horse Show–bound

I stared at the computer screen, trying to come up with an answer. After school I'd biked straight to Pat's Pets, where I have a part-time job on the Pet Help Line. My friend Catman

o's in eighth grade, answers the cat
another friend, Eddy Barker, who's in
rade with me but is way more respon-
bes the dog questions. He also works
me, helping Pat in the pet shop.
get any e-mails to do with horses. Pat trusts
ne on the help line because I gentle horses in
real life, training them for their owners by figuring them out instead of bullying them.

I'd already handled eight horse e-mails that
afternoon, but this one had me stumped.

March had come in like a lion. It was only
midmonth, but she was going out like a lamb.
Through Pat's window I could count 18 shades
of green. It even sounded like spring inside the
pet shop. Parrots squawked. Lovebirds sang.
New puppies yapped from their pen.

Catman slid over a crate to sit next to me.
He stared at my empty screen. He doesn't say
much, but he doesn't need to. We get each
other. In honor of spring Catman was wearing a
lime green leisure suit, which I guess guys wore
in the 70s. And a flowered shirt. Maybe it was
more like a flower-child shirt, like hippies used
to wear in the 60s. That's when Catman should
have lived. He would have fit right in.

Catman squinted at me through his wire-rimmed glasses, making his bright blue eyes piercing question marks.

"I know," I answered. "I just can't think of anything to tell somebody whose biggest problem is that her parents care too much about her life."

The truth was, I envied the kid. I only had one parent, and he'd been so tied up working on his current invention that lately we'd barely talked.

Note to self: Life is so unfair.

"Hang tight, Winnie," Catman advised, his eyes not letting me look away.

He knew. Somehow the Catman knew what I was thinking.

My mom had died almost three years ago, a week before my 10th birthday. We were living in Wyoming then so March was still winter. Even though there was a blizzard, I'd talked Mom into driving me to see the horse she was getting me for my birthday. That's when she had the accident. Birthdays weren't something I've looked forward to since then.

Dad was doing his best to raise my sister, Lizzy, and me. He'd quit his job with the insurance company in Laramie and moved us across the United States. We'd stopped for a few months in each of the *I* states—Illinois, Indiana, and Iowa—for my fifth and sixth grades before ending up in Ashland, Ohio.

We were making it too. Dad had turned into Odd-Job Willis, local handyman and inventor. And I'd become Winnie the Horse Gentler.

Only Dad's current invention had been taking over. It was almost like he wasn't even there. I guess Catman had noticed. He doesn't miss much.

Pat, the owner of the pet store, hollered up, "Catman! Can you help me with these itty-bitty kittens? If they're not the cat's meow! No offense." Pat always excuses herself to animals for using them in expressions.

Catman left and I typed my answer:

> Dear Horse Show—bound,
>   All I can say is that you should be really grateful that you have two parents who love you enough to embarrass you.
>   —Winnie the Horse Gentler

The bell over the pet-shop door rang, and Kaylee Hsu walked in. She glanced around, then waved when she spotted me.

Kaylee is as short as I am. But on her it looks good. She has shiny dark hair and a smile that makes you feel like you know her. If she were a horse, she'd be an easygoing Morgan. I guess she and her parents are Chinese-American, but they must have been in America longer than my relatives, because her English is 100 times better than mine.

I liked Kaylee. But we'd never really done much together. Her parents come to everything at school, and her mom is always the first to volunteer. I was pretty sure they have a lot of money, but Kaylee never acts stuck-up or anything—unlike Summer Spidell, another girl in our seventh-grade class. Summer's dad owns half of Ashland, and Summer acts like she owns the other half.

Kaylee stopped to talk to Pat. All week at school Kaylee had been going on and on about her horse, a buckskin she called Bandit. She didn't really own the gelding. But every spring, as soon as the old trail-riding stable just outside of town opened, she got her parents to go for an hour horseback ride with her. And for the past three years she'd always ridden the same horse.

Happy Trails was opening for their first ride

of the season Saturday—tomorrow—and Kaylee wanted me to go meet her horse today.

"Be right there!" I called, logging off. I said a quick good-bye to Pat and Catman, and left with Kaylee.

We biked the two miles to Happy Trails. Kaylee's bike is regular. Mine is a back bike, one of Dad's earliest inventions. I have to pedal backwards to go forward. I hate my bike because of the way people stare at me.

"I can't wait to see Bandit!" Kaylee said for the 100th time. "I go to that old livery for only one reason. Bandit. Wait until you see him, Winnie. They call him Buck, because he's a buckskin. But I've always called him Bandit. The first time I rode him, he stole a Snickers out of my back pocket and ate it, paper and all." She grinned sheepishly at me. "And now he has stolen my heart. I know it's silly. But for almost three years, I've pretended Bandit is mine."

I knew how Kaylee felt. I'd felt the same way about my horse, the most beautiful Arabian in the world. I'd dreamed of owning Nickers when people were still calling her Wild Thing. "It's not silly at all, Kaylee."

"I knew you would understand, Winnie."

When Happy Trails came into view, it surprised me how run-down the place was. Weeds hid half the hand-painted letters on the Happy Trails sign. Beer and pop cans littered the hill.

"I've never seen it this dilapidated," Kaylee said.

We left the bikes and walked up the lane, dodging puddles. About 10 horses' lengths from the stable was an old house. Both buildings had plywood nailed to the roof where shingles should have been. I had a feeling the stable had been nice once, log-cabin style, with hitching posts, like a Pony Express outpost. But now it was a rotten place for a horse to live. I thought about Stable-Mart, the ritzy stable owned by Summer Spidell's dad. What a difference!

Note to self: Life is so unfair for horses too.

It didn't look like anybody was around as I followed Kaylee into the stable. Inside it was dark and dank, and my first impulse was to set the prisoners free. The stalls were so small I wondered if the horses could even lie down or turn around in them.

Kaylee was already peeking into stalls. "Bandit?" she called.

7

When my eyes got used to the dark, I walked up to the first horse, an old Palomino. She was swatting flies with her tail. I hadn't seen a single fly at my barn. I'd thought it was too early for them. The mare didn't look up, even when I clicked for her. Her trough was empty, and I didn't see a water bucket. The manure had piled on the floor so long that it smelled like acid and vinegar.

"This is the mare Mom rode last year," Kaylee said, stopping two stalls down from me.

"It's great your mom rides with you," I said, trying not to think about the way my mom and I used to ride together.

"It's so dark in here!" Kaylee complained. "Bandit?"

I counted eight horses in the barn. At the next stall a roan Quarter Horse hung his head, as listless as the Palomino.

"Here you are, Bandit!" Kaylee cried. "It's me, Kaylee!"

I'd started down to Kaylee, when all of a sudden she screamed.

There was a crash, as if the horse had kicked down the stall.

"Kaylee!" I cried, running to her. "Are you okay?"

The back stall was even darker than the others. But I could make out a cream-colored horse that might have been a buckskin. He had his ears back and teeth bared.

"Bandit," Kaylee pleaded, approaching the stall again, "don't you remember me?"

"Be careful," I warned. The gelding's eyes were white with fear and anger. He looked too sweaty for the cool of the barn. His ribs and bony back stuck out, and I could smell his fear.

"I have to get closer," I said, feeling for the stall latch, as rage burned inside me. I could make out tiny scars on his rump and sides. It didn't take much imagination to picture the whip and spurs that had made those marks.

"Kaylee," I said, gripping the stall door so hard I felt splinters under my fingernails, "this horse has been abused."

$\mathcal{M}$y fingers closed around the stall latch, and I turned the handle.

"Here! You kids! Get away from there!"

The screechy voice sounded like fingernails on a chalkboard.

I ran to the door to see who was yelling. An old woman, thin and round-backed, hobbled out onto the porch of the broken-down house. She wore a winter coat and had a gray scarf tied over her gray hair. Even from a distance, I could see that her face would have been at home on a Wild West wanted poster.

"Go on, now!" she shouted. "This is private property!"

"Let's go!" Kaylee whispered.

I knew she was right. But I couldn't stand to leave Bandit.

"I'm going right now to call the police!" The woman turned and shuffled toward her door.

"Let's get out of here!" Kaylee insisted. "Winnie! We could get in trouble!" She grabbed my elbow and dragged me out of the barn, as the woman slammed the door of her run-down house.

Kaylee and I biked straight to my house for help. We hopped off our bikes and rolled them up the ditch and onto the lawn. Since the snow had melted, our muddy appliance graveyard was in full view again. Appliance parts spread across the lawn, as if a spring rain had showered us with metal. Dad uses the parts to repair things.

Instead of asking why we had junk all over our lawn, Kaylee said, "I like your house, Winnie. It's nice."

"It's not really ours," I admitted. I leaned my bike against a tree, and Kaylee leaned hers on the other side of the trunk. "We rent from Pat Haven. When we moved in, none of us thought we'd have any use for the barn or the pasture. Then I got Nickers. Then people started asking me to train their horses."

We made our way to the house, and I opened the door for her.

She stopped in the doorway, one hand on the door. "Winnie, I can't get Bandit out of my head. Do you think we should report Happy Trails to the animal protection people?"

"Maybe," I answered. "We can see what Dad thinks."

The screen door slammed behind us. "Dad!" I shouted.

I raced down the hall and into the living room. When I saw who was there, I stopped so suddenly that Kaylee ran into me. Madeline Edison and Dad were sitting on the couch. They'd met at the Chicago Invention Convention, where Madeline won some big prize. For months, they'd been spending time together—too much time, if you ask me. But, of course, nobody did.

Dad quickly removed his arm from around Madeline's shoulder. "Winnie! Didn't expect you home so soon."

I was sure Dad had no idea where I'd been or when to expect me home.

Madeline finger-waved at us. She was wearing a yellow flowered dress that might have looked pretty on somebody half her age.

"Who's your friend?" Dad asked, as if I hadn't just caught him with his arm around Madeline.

"Kaylee Hsu." I imagined frost clouds around my words.

"Hello, Mr. Willis," Kaylee said.

Dad introduced Madeline as his friend. Then he pointed behind our old couch. "And this is Mason."

I crossed the room to look behind the couch. Mason was lying on his back, staring at the ceiling. His eyes seemed focused on something the rest of us couldn't see.

Mason is Madeline's seven-year-old son. If you didn't know better, you'd think Mason and his mom were from different families or different planets. Madeline is tall and skinny, with wild red hair. Mason is small and blond. He looks more like five than seven.

They're different in other ways too. Madeline is supposed to be some kind of genius inventor. Mason goes to a school for kids with special needs.

"Hey, Mason," I said, squatting at the end of the couch. "What's going on?"

He didn't move. He didn't blink. I knew he hadn't heard me.

Sometimes Mason is just like a regular kid, only nicer, sweeter. But he can have these spells, or time-outs, when he shuts out the world. I admire that and wish I could do it myself. But it always makes me sad when Mason does it.

Dad and Madeline stood up. "Girls, maybe you should play outside," Dad said.

"Play outside?" I repeated. What were we, three-year-olds?

"I think it's best to leave Mason alone for a while," Madeline suggested. "Your father was about to show me what he's working on." She headed for Dad's workshop, and Dad trailed along.

"Dad!" I called. "I need to talk to you. Kaylee and I were at Happy Trails and—!"

"That's good, Winnie. Have a good time." He didn't even turn around. "Nice to meet you, Kaylee." He and Madeline disappeared into the workshop and closed the door.

I tried to shrug it off. "Dad's really caught up in his invention. Otherwise he would have helped."

Kaylee smiled, but I thought she looked sorry for me. I bet her dad never closed the door on her.

I turned away. It was hard not to see the house through Kaylee's eyes. She'd had to pass down the smudged hall and into the living room, where Lizzy had tried to hide the peeling, pale green walls under posters of tall pines and dense forests. At least Lizzy had picked up, because there wasn't a single newspaper on the gold carpet. But the thin spots on the shag showed under Dad's easy chair and the couch.

Kaylee glanced toward the couch. "What's wrong with the little boy?" she whispered.

I moved to the hall, in case Mason really could hear me. "Mason's not always like this. You'll have to meet him when he's having a good day. He's the cutest kid in the world. Loves horses too. He's the one I gave the foal to—the one that was born on Christmas Day."

She nodded and waited for me to go on.

"Something happened to Mason when he was a baby. I'm not sure what. I think Dad knows, but he won't tell me. Madeline won't talk about it. But Mason's head was injured. It left him with neur . . . neur . . ." I tried to think of the word Dad had used.

"Neurological damage?" Kaylee asked.

"That's it. Kind of like autism, but it's not."

"What can they do for him?" Kaylee asked, her whole face wrinkled in worry.

"When something sets him off, like somebody shouting or scaring him, Madeline says you just have to try to keep him from retreating from the world. She says they try to get Mason to see the world as a friendly place instead."

Kaylee and I moved to the kitchen and downed some of Lizzy's cheese cookies while we tried to figure out our next move. We thought about calling the animal-protection people. Kaylee was pretty sure we wanted the ASPCA, American Society for the Prevention of Cruelty to Animals, but we couldn't find their number in the Ashland County phone book. I tried calling Ralph Evans, who runs the local animal shelter, plus he gives the sermons at our church until we get a full-time pastor. But he was out of town for a wedding.

Finally we biked back to Pat's Pets to see if Pat had heard any complaints about Happy Trails.

Pat was paying bills at her desk by the boa constrictor, but she dropped everything to listen to us. Kaylee and I took turns telling her about Bandit and the gross barn.

"Are you gals talking about the Pulaski barn?" Pat asked, as if that surprised her. "Happy Trails?"

"That's what we've been telling you, Pat," I said.

"I went to school with the Pulaski girl, Karen. Real nice family. Animal lovers."

"Are you sure we're talking about the same place?" Kaylee asked.

"I lost touch when Karen moved to San Francisco. Haven't seen her mama in years. But I remember Mrs. Pulaski. Big woman. Used to take in stray cats. Squirrels too. I can't believe she'd mistreat any creature."

"Maybe she sold Happy Trails," I suggested, "to that mean old woman we saw."

"I don't believe I'd seen that woman before," Kaylee said. "Last year a rather large man with a disagreeable disposition ran the stable. My mother disliked him so intensely that she tried to coerce me into riding at Mohegan Stables instead."

Kaylee used bigger words when she talked to grown-ups. But I knew what she was saying.

Pat frowned. "Did this fella have teeny, tiny eyes and a nose that made you want to honk it?"

"I had no desire to honk his nose," Kaylee said. "But that does sound like the same man."

"Leonard," Pat muttered.

"You know him?" I asked.

"Karen's cousin from Red Haw. Neither of us ever did care much for that cousin of hers. Lazy Lenny we used to call him. If Mrs. Pulaski has Lenny working for her, she's probably doing a favor for her sister. But she would never let him hurt a horse."

"Well, something happened to Bandit," Kaylee said. "My parents and I are riding at Happy Trails tomorrow. Maybe I can find out more."

The phone rang. Barker answered it. "Kaylee!" he called. "It's for you!"

"Me?" Kaylee talked a minute on the phone, then came back. "Sorry. I have to go. I'd told Mom I'd be here, so she's coming by for me. She's taking me to Mansfield to get a gift for Summer's birthday party tomorrow." She gave me a sad smile. "I'm sorry, Winnie."

"That I didn't get invited?" I asked. "Don't be."

It's no secret that Summer and I don't exactly get along. I used to muck stalls at Spidells' Stable-Mart. I gave them a hard time for training and breaking horses instead of gentling them. True, it would have felt good to be invited, but I'm not sure I would have wanted to celebrate the birth of Summer Spidell.

A blue van pulled up in front of Pat's Pets.

"That's Mom," Kaylee said, heading for the door. "Thanks, Pat. Winnie, I'll pick up my bike and give you a full report tomorrow as soon as we get back from Happy Trails."

A lady came over to Pat and asked for help picking out a bunny for her daughter. Then the bell rang, and a mother and daughter walked in.

Pat took the bunny lady, and Barker met the mother-and-daughter team by the fish tanks. If I were a customer, I'd buy anything Barker suggested. He's got that kind of face. He also has a lot of other things going for him. Two great parents who teach African-American literature and art and stuff at Ashland University. And five little brothers who considered Barker their hero.

Note to self: Did I say life is so unfair?

Although I'd been fighting it for days, my

photographic memory kicked in. Most people think it sounds great to have a photographic memory, but they're wrong. My mind takes picture of things, even when I don't want it to. And I have no control over when the pictures will flash back.

That's what started happening as I watched Barker showing the mother and daughter golden retriever puppies. I shut my eyes, but I still saw my mom, the way she'd been when the car stopped rolling and I looked over at her. Her head lay against the steering wheel, and she wasn't moving, as snow pounded the windshield and the car shook in the high winds.

Outside the window of Pat's Pets, mothers and daughters, and mothers, fathers, and daughters were everywhere.

It felt like a conspiracy.

Waiting for Pat to finish with her customer,
I fiddled with paper clips on her desk. I moved
her magnets on the chipped gray filing cabinet.
Some of the magnets were animal-shaped.
Some of them had Bible verses.

One magnet was shaped like a teardrop. I read
the verse on it:

> *When others are happy, be happy with them.*
> *If they are sad, share their sorrow.*
> —Romans 12:15

Something twinged inside me, which is how
God gets my attention and makes me think
about stuff. *Okay, God,* I said in my head, which,
I guess, is praying. *I don't have any trouble being
sad when people are sad. But it's harder to be happy*

23

for kids who get to spend every day with their moms. Or kids like Horse Show–bound who have two parents who care enough to be embarrassing.

It was almost closing time, but more customers trickled in. I probably should have gone home. Lizzy would have dinner ready. She's a year younger than me, but a great cook, which is a good thing because Dad and I don't cook.

But I didn't feel like going home. Madeline might still be there, for one thing. And Lizzy was having her friend Geri spend the night, so all conversation would be about reptiles and amphibians. My sister loves lizards, and her friend is nuts about frogs. Sometimes I wonder what it would be like to have a real best friend like that.

Catman Coolidge strolled out from the back of the store, waved me the peace sign, and plopped down at the computer. I ambled over and took a seat on the crate. He logged on to the Web site, keying in letters and numbers so fast, it looked like he was using all of his fingers to type instead of just his thumbs and pinkies.

Dear Catman,
    I want a Siamese cat. My aunt says
I can have one of the kittens from her

cat's litter. But if you ask me, something's fishy. None of the kittens have
black or brown markings, like the
mother cat. They're all plain. You think
my aunt is trying to put one over on
me?
—Siamese Fan

Catman started typing his answer before I'd
finished reading the question.

Dear Siamese Fan,
    Chill, Daddy-O! Don't be bummed
by plain Janes. All Siamese kittens are
born without markings. You dig? Little
cats get markings later. And the more
you handle your kitten, the sooner it
will get markings. I kid you not!
—The Catman

I kept watching, and Catman kept answering:

Dear Catman,
    My parents FiNALLY said I could
have my own cat, even though I'm
kinda allergic to them. We're buying
a shorthaired cat. Any other advice?
—Sneezing in Strongsville

Dear Sneezing,

Get a white cat, man! Cats with light hair are six times less likely to trigger allergies than cats with black hair. Easy, dude.

—The Catman

Dear Catman,

Tomorrow, for my birthday, I get to pick out any kitten I want from the animal shelter. Any tips for me?

—Birthday Boy

I couldn't believe it. Was everybody having a birthday? Catman was already answering.

Happy birthday, Man!

Gnarly gift! A cat is a cat, from day one. That kitty's personality won't change once you get him home. The first kitten who runs to you will end up bossing your pad. He might fight other pets, scratch sofas, and scratch you if you don't give the dude enough attention. The shy kitty may never like being cuddled.

Watch the cats. Do they make nice

together? When a kitten hears a loud noise, does he get scared and run to Mommy, or just look around then play it cool? What you see is what you get. Have a blast!

—The Catman

Pat bustled over to us. "I'll be a monkey's uncle—no offense—if this isn't the busiest day we've had in a spell!" She put her hand on my shoulder. "So, Winnie, how's your science-fair project coming?" Pat had been our "temporary" life science teacher since the first day of school. She was also the chairperson of our school's science fair.

I shrugged. I hadn't felt like doing a project. We didn't have to do one, although just about everybody was. And I could have used the extra credit.

"Monday's the last day to get your outline in," Pat warned. "Love your invention, Catman!"

"What are you inventing?" I asked, surprised. Catman's really smart, but not much of a joiner. "Aren't you protesting science on behalf of Felines Against Fems?" It had something to do with cosmetic experiments on cats.

"The protest is solid," Catman explained. "Nothing to do with the science fair, though. I'm down with cool-cat bunks—bunk beds for cats."

Barker whizzed by, carrying a big box. "Catman was going to make a portable eight-track player. I talked him out of it. Time to let it go, man."

"Your project is a hoot, Barker!" Pat exclaimed. "Tell Winnie about it."

"Dog greeting cards," Barker explained, juggling his box. "People can send the cards to their pets, and the dogs can eat the whole thing. It's good for them."

"I'm thinking I might carry some of Barker's dog cards right here in the store," Pat said. "So Winnie, what kind of scientific wonder are you creating?"

I sighed. "I don't think I'm entering the science fair, Pat. I can't think of anything good."

"Winnie Willis!" Pat is almost as short as I am, which is too short. But she's a force—small as a Welsh Cob and just as powerful. Her big, brown eyes screamed disapproval. "You could get your grade back up to an A with the extra points."

I would have liked that. Pat's class was my favorite. It would have been my only A.

I shook my head. "It's too late. I couldn't put an invention together in a week."

"Are you kidding?" Pat asked. "Why, sure you could, what with that inventor father of yours! He can help, you know. Long as you do the lion's share of the inventing. No offense." Pat nodded to the cats.

"Dad's too busy to help," I mumbled.

"To help with an invention?" Pat asked. "I'll bet he'd drop everything to work on an invention with you!"

I stared at Pat. I'd never even once thought about that. This wasn't like asking him to help me with math or English. This was an invention. And my dad loves inventions.

"You think so, Pat? He's awful tied up with this temperature suit he's working on."

"Of course he'll want to help you invent something!" Pat exclaimed. "I guarantee it, Winnie. You scoot on home and ask him right now. I need that outline Monday!"

I glanced over at Catman. He nodded.

Maybe they were right. Dad lived for inventions. Why wouldn't he want to invent something with me? Pat thought so. Even Catman thought so.

I raced out of the shop and hopped onto my back bike. A man getting into his car stopped to stare as I pedaled backwards and moved onto the street. But I didn't feel embarrassed. The back bike seemed different. There was something about it. It was a pretty good invention, now that I thought about it.

My dad was an inventor. Why couldn't I come up with something great for the science fair? Especially with a real inventor father to help. I already had some horse-related ideas. Dad and I could work on them together.

I pictured my dad at the science fair, looking on proudly. He'd probably even cheer loud enough to embarrass me.

I could hardly wait to get home and get started.

$\mathcal{M}$adeline's car was gone when I got home. Good. Less competition for Dad. I dropped my bike on the lawn and trotted into the house, practicing in my head how I'd ask for his help. I tried to think like Lizzy, who could talk anybody into anything.

"Hi, Winnie!" Lizzy called.

I kicked off my muddy tennis shoes, then found my sister in the kitchen, stirring something in a big bowl. A lot of people think Lizzy and I look alike, which is a huge compliment to me because Lizzy is beautiful. She has zero freckles to my 23. And her hair never looks like it's exploded from her head.

"Hey, Lizzy. Where's Dad?"

"Workshop, of course." Lizzy wrinkled her

31

nose in the direction of the garage, which Dad had transformed into a workshop. "Wouldn't go there if I were you."

Just as she said it, a crash came from the workshop, then a growl that had to have come from Dad, since we don't own bears.

"The temperature suit?" I asked.

Lizzy nodded. "Space heater's on full force. Dad could invent the sauna in there."

The "temp suit" was a one-piece suit that changed colors with the changing weather. I wasn't anxious for Dad to finish, since he was making it size small. And that meant I'd have to try it out, maybe even wear it to school. Lizzy's a medium. Dad is size long and tall.

I sank to the kitchen table and forced myself to wait until Dad stopped banging things.

"I'll cut you a slice of popcorn bread," Lizzy offered.

The whole kitchen smelled like popcorn. It's my third favorite smell, right behind horse and horse manure.

Lizzy brought me a thick slice of crunchy, white bread, loaded with butter. My sister is a natural in the kitchen, the way I am in the barn. I got my horse sense from our mom, who was the best horse gentler in Wyoming. I'm not sure where Lizzy got her cooking skills, though. Mom hated to cook.

While we ate, I tried out some of my invention ideas on Lizzy. "What do you think about horse-scent air freshener? If I could get the smell of horse into an aerosol can, wouldn't that be great?"

"Sweet, Winnie!" Lizzy could be a cheerleader. "What else?"

"I've always wanted to see the world like a horse does. I've told you how horses can see 350 degrees around them, everywhere except a spot in front and behind. Well, what if Dad and I sewed rearview mirrors around a baseball cap so you could see in every direction like a horse? I could call it the 'horse hat.'"

"You rock!" Lizzy shouted.

The front door slammed. "I'm here!" It was Geri, Lizzy's friend, who never bothers to knock. Geri's blonde, and Lizzy's more like brunette. But they both have green eyes and are almost exactly the same height.

"In here, Geri!" Lizzy called.

Geri barreled into the kitchen and flung her sleeping bag on the floor. "Hi, Winnie. Did Lizzy tell you we're sleeping outside tonight?"

"I think it's supposed to rain," I said.

"No problem!" Geri unwrapped her sleeping bag. She pulled a string, and up popped a row of small umbrellas that spread the length of the rolled-out bag. "See? Lizzy collected broken umbrellas, fixed them, and sewed them to our sleeping bags. They're like a built-in tent, in case it rains."

"Does it work?" I asked. But it did look like the bag would stay dry. The umbrellas overlapped, covering the whole thing.

"Guess we'll find out tonight," Lizzy said, clearing the table. She grabbed three tomatoes from the fridge and tossed one to Geri and one to me for a snack. "Good luck with Dad, Winnie!"

Geri and Lizzy ran outside, giggling and bumping each other.

I ate my tomato with salt, then walked to the workshop and pressed my ear against the door. The banging had stopped. I knocked.

No answer.

I stuck my head in. "Dad?"

Dad was cutting something on the worktable. He turned toward me briefly, then back to the table. "Hello, Winnie. I'm in the middle of something. If I can . . ." His voice trailed off as he worked the material with giant scissors.

"I just need to ask you something, Dad," I tried.

"Could we do it later, honey? This invention is driving me crazy. I—ow!" He dropped the scissors and stuck his little finger in his mouth.

"It'll just take a second, Dad. Actually, what I want to talk to you about is an invention."

"Uh-huh." He turned his back on me, picked up the scissors, and started cutting again.

"At school they're having a science fair. And each kid is supposed to come up with an invention. And there's a competition. And the winner goes to Columbus for the state finals."

"Winnie, will you hand me that curling iron?" Dad asked, sticking out his hand behind him.

I handed him the curling iron.

"So," I continued, "there's not much time to get ready. But if we worked together, well, we could do it."

There was no sound except the hum of the space heater and the swish of the scissors.

"So, would you?" I asked.

Dad set down the scissors and turned around.

He looked at me like I had a third eye. "Would I what?"

"Help me with the project?"

Dad frowned. "Winnie, you have to do your own schoolwork. I'm a little rusty in seventh-grade subjects. Besides, I'm up to my elbows in my own project. I'm sorry, honey. Maybe Lizzy can help. Or Catman?" He smiled at me like I was a two-year-old who had just asked him to take me to the playground. Then he turned back to his own work.

I stared holes through his back. Pat Haven was wrong. Catman was wrong. I was wrong. And I should have known better.

"Fine." I spit out the word and left, slamming the door behind me.

I ran to the barn, slipping twice in the mud. I was breathing hard, not from running but from holding in tears. *It's not fair,* I muttered to God. *Every other kid in my school has parents helping them with science projects! But not me. Not my dad, the inventor.*

I inhaled the smell of horse and manure. It's my sure cure for any problem. But it wasn't working. My temper had exploded, and I couldn't get it back in. Mom used to call me her "hot-tempered Mustang." I was living up to the name.

I walked into Nickers' stall. She and Buddy, the orphan filly, still shared the same stall, even though Buddy was almost three months old now. Nickers had taken over as adopted mom. Next to them was Annie Goat, on loan from

37

Granny Barker, Eddy Barker's great-grandmother. The goat had been a lifesaver for Buddy, who had nursed from Annie before learning to drink from a bucket.

The rest of the barn was empty except for my friend Hawk's horse, Towaco. It had been a month since I'd boarded my last problem horse, a Miniature Falabella, who belonged to one of my classmates, Sal. The Mini had moved to the backyard of Sal's grandmother. I had two problem horses lined up for April and May. But for now the barn felt empty.

I scratched Buddy's chest, then threw my arms around Nickers' strong, white neck. She nickered softly, and I felt her vibrate. She turned her elegant Arabian head toward me and pressed her dish jowl against my head. Sometimes it seemed like Nickers was the only good thing in my life.

"I need a ride, girl."

I slipped on the bitless hackamore, even though sometimes I just ride with the halter and lead. But the March wind was blowing. I knew Nickers would be feeling her oats. I led her out of the stall, then jumped up bareback. She and Buddy whinnied back and forth.

Then we were off. Nickers set out at a canter across the pasture. The jarring of the earth helped wear down my anger. I shut out all sound except the pounding of hooves. There was no one but Nickers and me.

We jumped a log, trotted down a ravine and up another one. I let her go wherever she wanted. Leaning onto her neck, I wrapped my arms around her and tried to put every thought out of my head. Part of me wanted to pray because I felt so lousy, but the other part of me felt so lousy I couldn't pray.

I shut my eyes and pretended I was back in Wyoming.

We cantered on and on. I wanted to get as far away as possible from Dad's workshop.

When we were both spent, Nickers and I took our time walking back. The sky had turned gray, and the clouds looked bottom heavy. I felt like riding over to Kaylee's, but I knew she'd still be out shopping for Summer's birthday present.

Note to self: Birthdays. Bah humbug.

Summer and I weren't the only ones having

birthdays. Lizzy's birthday was coming up too—March 23, the day before mine. For one day each year, Lizzy and I are the same age. Poor Lizzy. I hadn't heard her mention her birthday. I guess I'd ruined birthdays for both of us.

Note to self: Write your congressman about banning birthdays. Everyone over 30 would vote for it.

I rode through the pasture and came up the back way to the barn. Buddy was waiting for us in the paddock. She came trotting out of the stall, whinnying her high-pitched squeal.

Nickers answered with a long neigh that shook me.

I slid off Nickers' back. "Come on, you two. Let's get you and Towaco fed."

"There they are!" Mason Edison waved from the barn. He looked okay again. Even from the paddock I could see his dimple. As if God were reaching down and poking long fingers through the clouds, sunlight leaked onto Mason in white-yellow streaks.

Buddy trotted to him. I had a feeling that being with Buddy had snapped Mason back into our world. When the filly's mother died in my barn, Mason had been so upset that I ended up giving him the foal. It had been the right thing to do. Mason and Buddy had come alive for each other over the past couple of months.

There's a term in horse training called *join up*. It means that a horse and a human create a bond, joining each other in the same world— part horse, part human. Buddy and Mason had joined up. They both seemed happiest when they were in the same world.

"Hey, Mason!" I shouted.

"My Buddy," Mason said, hugging her. Mason is the one who gave the filly the name Buddy. Not your usual girl name, but it fits.

Madeline Edison scurried out of the way as Nickers and Buddy trotted past her to the stalls. "Hello, Winnie." She looked more normal now too. Her moods seemed to flip back and forth in time with her son's. "We were all the way home when Mason turned to me and announced that he wanted to see Buddy." She grinned.

I grinned back. Loving Mason was the one thing Madeline and I had in common, if you didn't count the fact that we both like my dad. And I, for one, did not count that fact.

"We were just going in to see your father. Are you coming?" she asked.

"No. Barn chores," I said, not mentioning that

seeing my dad was about the last thing I wanted. "Mason can help me if he wants."

Mason turned his big-eyed hopeful look on his mom. It worked.

"All right." She reached down and stroked his white-blond hair. "Just be careful."

She walked off toward the house, saying, "I'm quite anxious to see how Jack's project is coming."

My anger bubbled up again. Maybe it was the mention of Dad's project. Or maybe it was hearing Madeline call my dad "Jack." My mom called him "Jack."

"Come on, Mason," I said, going to the tack box. "Let's groom Buddy."

I took out the filly's halter and picked the softest brush. Mason slipped on Buddy's halter with no problem. Dad had given me the halter for Christmas. It seemed like a year ago, a time when he really cared about things. We'd all known how sick Buddy's mother was and how little chance there was that she or her foal would make it through the birth. Yet Dad had cared enough to buy me a halter for a foal he didn't think would survive.

Mason tied the filly by her grain trough. We'd

been doing this for weeks, just to get her used to being tied. He brushed Buddy while I fed Towaco and Nickers and mucked stalls.

Towaco, Hawk's blanket-patterned Appaloosa, nuzzled me as I sprinkled fresh straw in his stall. He'd been an angel since Hawk had brought him back from Florida. She'd spent her Christmas break there at her dad's new home.

Hawk and I liked to ride together whenever we could. But she hadn't had much time lately. Her mom had been taking her to Mansfield Photo Studio a couple of times a week. I didn't know why, and I didn't ask. Hawk usually did whatever she thought either parent wanted.

I was helping Mason clean out Buddy's hooves when I heard someone running into the barn.

"Winnie?" It was Dad.

I dropped Buddy's hoof and unbuckled his halter. "Dad? What's wrong?" It had to be bad to get him out of his workshop. I ran out to meet him, a million horrible scenes flashing through my head, most of them starring Lizzy.

"Madeline said you were here."

"What is it?" I tried to breathe and stop the pictures in my head.

"I couldn't wait for you to come back! Did you say *invention*?"

"What are you talking about?" I asked, feeling my lungs untwist.

"An invention! Your invention. I was so caught up in the workshop I hardly heard you. Then after you left, I started to replay it. And I was sure you said you wanted to invent something. I asked Lizzy, and she told me about the science fair. And I get to help?"

"I thought you were too busy," I said. I wanted to stay mad at him. But he was so wide-eyed, he reminded me of a colt.

"Too busy to invent with you? Are you serious? Winnie, this could be the start of something big!"

"You want to help?" I asked, afraid maybe we still weren't understanding each other.

"Of course I'll help! We're going to come up with the best ever Willis invention! Willis and Willis! Come on! Let's start right now!"

I grinned at Dad, and he grinned back. It felt like more eye contact than we'd had in weeks.

Then we walked to the house, my dad's arm around my shoulder. He didn't even wave good-bye to Madeline.

$\mathcal{F}$or the next hour Dad and I sat at the kitchen table, plotting my invention for the science fair. Actually, I sat. Dad kept popping up, as if he had springs for legs. Each idea set him off like a Jack-Willis-in-the-box.

I told Dad about the horse hat and the horse-scent air freshener. He jumped up for both ideas, but they didn't have wide enough "crowd appeal," he said.

Dad paced while I stared at the box of sugar-substitute packets Lizzy keeps on the table for Dad's coffee. "Hey! How about fake sugar cubes?" I suggested. "Horses love sugar, but it's bad for their teeth."

Dad sprang out of his seat but dropped back into it, frowning. "Too many patents involved."

I was running out of ideas, but I didn't want to let Dad down. "What about a hoof pick that's regular on one end, but—"

Dad didn't even bother to spring up. "Breadth, Winnie. Think crowd appeal."

I thought *crowd appeal,* but it didn't help.

We sat in silence so long that I had to fight my eyelids to keep them from shutting. I'm sure the wheels were whirring in Dad's brain, but mine had shut down.

Outside, wind blew branches against the kitchen window. Raindrops plinked, then pelted the roof. I hoped Lizzy and Geri were keeping dry. I thought about Kaylee's Buckskin Bandit and hoped he was safe for the night. My stomach hurt just thinking about it.

"Dad," I said at last when I couldn't herd my wild thoughts. "Is it okay if I take my shower? Could we pick this up in the morning?"

Dad's mouth sagged, but he said, "Sure. Maybe we need to sleep on it."

I hung a washcloth on the bathroom doorknob, our way of alerting people that the bathroom's occupied. The lock had been broken for months. I ran hot water into the tub. We really just have a bathtub, not a shower. But Dad had rigged a shower hose.

I turned the dial and waited for the water to shoot through the hose. Then I held it over my head and pretended it was a real shower. I wanted to wash away most of the day—every thought about birthdays and abused horses. The only pictures I wanted to hang on to were my ride with Nickers and the look on Dad's face when he'd come into the barn to tell me he wanted us to be the Willis and Willis invention team.

"How was the shower?" Dad asked when I came out in pj's, my head wrapped in a towel.

I sighed. "I wish we had a real shower, with 10 nozzles that could spray me at the same time."

Dad sprang from his easy chair. "Eureka!"

"Huh?"

"Eureka! It's what the Greek mathematician Archimedes cried over 2,100 years ago when he landed onto an earthshaking discovery! 'Eureka! I found it!'"

"I know what it means, Dad. Why did you say it?"

"Winnie, you are following in the footsteps of the great! And both discoveries sprouted in the fertile soil of an ordinary bathtub. Amazing!"

I wasn't getting any of this. "Dad—?"

"We'll assemble a Magnificent Multishower! Ten shower heads—no, 12—running up and down the shower stall on all four sides." Dad paced in a tight circle. He reminded me of a nervous Thoroughbred.

I couldn't imagine bringing a shower into our school gym. Besides, it didn't have anything to do with horses. "You know, Dad, I was just saying that stuff about the shower because my arm got tired holding up our hose."

But Dad was in another world. "Junkyard. Warehouse. Army supply. Cold water, hot water."

"Maybe we should sleep on it?" I suggested.

Dad turned wide eyes on me. Sal, my classmate who owns Amigo, the Mini, says she thinks my dad is handsome for an old person. I guess his big brown eyes and black curly hair are his best features. But tonight they gave him a wild, lion-tamer look. "This is it, Winnie! We will invent the Multishower!"

I still thought it was a dumb idea. But I was so tired I would have agreed to invent another Summer Spidell. Although I might have tried for a nice version.

"Okay, Dad." I yawned. "We'll get on it first thing in the morning."

"Morning?" Dad laughed like a mad scientist. "First rule of invention: Strike while the iron's hot! To the workshop, Winnie! There's work to be done!"

I followed Dad to the chilly workshop and listened as he rattled off plans and schedules. He didn't seem to notice as the shop grew colder and I grew sleepier.

I don't know what time we stopped working because when I woke up, daylight was streaming through my bedroom window and I was in bed. Dad must have carried me there. The last thing I remembered was Dad whistling "There Shall Be Showers of Blessing."

Lizzy's bed hadn't been slept in. Her half of the room looked like a tornado had blown everything over to my half, leaving hers neat and clean, and mine jumbled. I hoped she and Geri hadn't gotten drenched in the backyard.

I threw on jeans and a sweatshirt and stumbled to the kitchen. Lizzy had left me a note:

Winnie, we let you sleep. Dad said you were up late inventing. Geri and I are going down by the creek to see if the snakes are out yet. Help yourself to muffins. —Love, Lizzy

P.S. Lizzy and I stayed dry as a bone in our sleeping-bag tents. —Geri

I bit into a cornflake muffin.

The phone rang. Before I could answer it, Dad zoomed in from the workshop and grabbed the receiver. "Willis and Willis Inventors." He squinted at me and pointed to the workshop. Interpretation: Get to work!

"Hello, Hawk," Dad said.

I started for the phone, but Dad waved me off.

"I'm afraid Winnie can't ride today. We're working on Winnie's invention."

"Dad!" I held out my hand for the receiver.

"I think Winnie wants to talk to you for a second." Dad raised his eyebrows as he handed over the phone.

For a month I'd been griping because Dad didn't want to spend time with me. I couldn't desert him now, even though I would have loved to ride with Hawk. "Guess I can't ride today, Hawk," I said into the phone.

"I heard," Hawk said. "Just as well, I suppose. Mother wants more publicity photos."

"What's she do with all those pictures?" My dad never even bought the school's photo packages.

"Mother dreams of making me into a model." Hawk didn't sound like she shared the dream.

"Does she know you're 13?"

Hawk laughed. "According to my mother, 13 is prime for catalog models. I am waiting for her to outgrow this modeling fantasy. Sounds like your dad has a new dream too. Willis and Willis Inventors?"

"Don't ask," I said. "Are you doing a project for the science fair?"

"Yes. But it is not very inventive. Mother takes all my free time with these trips to the studio. All I have come up with is—do not laugh—bird diapers."

In the background, I heard squawking, then *"Ring, ring! Hello?"* I recognized Peter Lory,

Hawk's chattering lory, an Indonesian parrot
with a good vocabulary. The real Peter Lorre
was an actor who played gangsters in old crime
movies Hawk watches on late-night TV.

"Peter doesn't sound too happy about your
invention," I commented.

"He hates the diaper. The parakeets are good
sports, though. And mother does not mind so
much when they fly around the house if they
wear diapers."

"Winnie!" Dad shouted from the workshop.

"I have to go, Hawk."

"See you Monday."

The second I hung up, the phone ran again.
I snatched it up, thinking Hawk had forgotten
something. "Hawk?"

"Madeline. Hello, Winnie. Is your father
home?"

I thought about saying no. Technically, the
workshop wasn't home really. "He's in the
workshop," I admitted. "We're pretty busy."

We didn't speak for a second. Then she said,
"May I speak with him, please?"

I thought about saying no. Dad wouldn't have
let me talk to Hawk if I hadn't been in the
room. "Okay."

I jogged to the workshop. "Dad, Madeline's on the phone. Should I tell her you're too busy to—?"

He brushed past me in his rush for the phone. "Winnie, see if you can get those screws out of the shower door while I talk to Madeline."

"Okay. But I have to do barn chores first."

"All done," Dad said, picking up the phone.

"What?"

"I asked Lizzy to do them so we could get down to business."

"Our Lizzy did barn chores?" Lizzy would happily hold snakes, lizards, and bugs. But she sweats if she gets within 10 feet of a horse.

"She wasn't crazy about the idea," Dad admitted. "But once I explained our urgency with your invention, she agreed to help. Geri too."

Unbelievable.

For the rest of the morning Dad and I raided junkyards, which Dad called "discovery centers." We found hoses and showerheads, not to mention dead raccoons and live skunks.

Dad kept up a steady stream of dialogue. "Did you know, Winnie, that in the 1500s, whole families bathed in a single tub of water? The man of the house got to bathe first. Then he left his water for his wife's bath. When she finished, the children took turns in order of their ages. Last, the baby was given a bath. Hence the expression 'Don't throw the baby out with the bathwater.' We have come a long way, but you and I are about to bring the American family the rest of the way."

Back in the workshop, Dad kept me busy cleaning showerheads. He answered all phone calls. We didn't even break for lunch. Lizzy and Geri brought in lime milk shakes and fried-egg sandwiches.

It wasn't until Dad was wedged behind the shower stall, blowtorch in hand, that I was able to escape the workshop. The phone rang, and I dashed out to get it before he could stop me.

"Hello?"

"Winnie! Where have you been? And how can you not have an answering machine?"

"Kaylee? I've been waiting for you to call. How's—"

"Me? You were supposed to call *me* back! I've been waiting all day. Didn't your dad tell you?"

"He's so into this invention stuff he must have forgotten." But I knew Dad hadn't told me on purpose. "I'm sorry, Kaylee. Go on! What happened at Happy Trails?"

"Winnie, it was awful!" Kaylee broke down. I could hear her choking on her tears. "Bandit wasn't there. And, Winnie, they said the buckskin never existed!"

$\mathcal{K}$aylee's words echoed over the receiver:
"They said the buckskin never existed."

"W-wait," I stammered. "Who said Bandit
didn't exist?"

"The big man with the honking nose!"

"Leonard?" I asked, remembering what Pat
had said about Lazy Lenny.

"He's a horrible man, Winnie! He acted like
I was crazy. Then he brought out this horse
that was kind of the same color as Bandit, but
it wasn't Bandit. And my parents believed him!
They couldn't tell the difference."

I didn't like it that Leonard would lie about the
horse and say the buckskin never existed. If he'd
sold Bandit, why wouldn't he have just said so?

"Winnie, I'm at Summer's. For her party, you

know. Will you come get me? I have to go back to Happy Trails and look for Bandit."

"Winnie!" Dad shouted from the workshop.

"Kaylee, I don't know if I can—"

"Please, Winnie!" She sounded so desperate.

"Hang on. I'll be right there."

It wasn't easy to convince Dad to give me a break from inventing. I had to promise to work all night if he needed me.

Lizzy and Geri were feeding Annie Goat when I walked into the barn.

"Is this goat always so crabby?" Geri asked.

"Pretty much," I answered. I took Nickers out, slipped on the hackamore, and swung up.

"Where are you going?" Lizzy asked. Her hair was in pigtails, and I don't think I'd ever seen it look worse. It still looked better than my hair, though.

"Summer's party. Thanks for helping out, you guys."

It didn't take long to reach Spidells' Stable-Mart. Nickers trotted up the long gravel drive past the sterile white barn. From inside came a *thud, thud*.

Probably Spidell's Sophisticated Scarlet Lady,
Summer's million-dollar horse. Scar, my pet name
for the exotic American Saddle Horse, wins every
horse show Summer enters. But Summer and Scar
will never be friends the way Nickers and I are.

I rode closer to the house, hoping Kaylee was
watching for me.

Summer Spidell stepped outside, without letting go of the doorknob. "What do you want,
Winifred?" she shouted. Her blonde hair looked
like she'd just gotten out of the beauty salon.
Her yellow dress matched her hair. "Well? You're
leaving hoofprints on the lawn!"

"Oops. Wouldn't want to leave hoofprints at
a stable."

"Go!" She pointed toward my end of town, in
case I'd forgotten which side of the tracks I lived
on. "We're trying to have a party here."

"I know," I said. "I heard the bulletin on CNN."

She looked like she almost believed me.

"Summer!" Mrs. Spidell shouted. She stepped
out of the house, carrying a cake the size of
Tennessee. She smiled at me, then lowered
her voice to Summer. "We're cutting the cake,
sweetheart."

"Not yet, Mother!" Summer shot back.

"Winnie?" Hawk eased outside, as Summer and her mother disappeared into the house. Hawk's long black hair caught the sinking sun and threw it back in sparkles. She was wearing a fringed skirt that might have been Native American. Hawk and I love her Native American heritage, although neither of her parents is into it.

"Are you coming in?" Hawk asked.

I shook my head. "I just came by to talk to Kaylee."

"Victoria!" Summer called. She and her friends use Hawk's real name, Victoria Hawkins.

"I will send Kaylee out," Hawk said. She smiled, and I could see why her mother believed Hawk could make it as a model.

"Winnie!" Kaylee dashed out of the house, stumbling on the step. She ran up to Nickers. "I thought you'd never get here! My parents are picking me up in an hour, so that's all the time we have."

"Hop on behind me," I said, riding Nickers close to the step so she could climb aboard. "Let's get out of here."

It took three tries, but she made it.

"Hang on!" I said, urging Nickers to cut through the Spidells' yard.

The door slammed open behind us, and Summer Spidell let out a cry. Then she yelled after us, "Winifred! You come back here right now! Bring Kaylee back this minute!"

We could hear Summer hollering the whole time as we crossed the Spidell lawn and galloped out of town. It was the most fun I'd had all day.

On the ride over, Kaylee filled me in. "My parents and I were the first customers at Happy Trails." She had to shout over the wind. "There were only five horses in the barn, and Leonard told us we could pick from those. I told him I wanted to ride the buckskin, and that's when he brought out the wrong horse."

When Kaylee had insisted she wanted to see the other cream-colored horse, Leonard said that these five were the only horses they had at Happy Trails.

"I knew he was lying," Kaylee continued. "And when more customers drove up, he was caught in his lie. It was a family of four. And *voila!* Just like that, Leonard disappeared and came back with two more horses, so he could take money from all seven of us! But he still didn't bring out Bandit. That's why I'm sure my horse is still there."

Happy Trails looked deserted as we rode up the lane. I started to holler for somebody, but Kaylee put her hand over my mouth. "Don't!" she whispered. "Let's find Bandit ourselves."

I looped Nickers' reins over the hitching post and followed Kaylee into the stable. It seemed smellier and smaller than it had the day before.

Kaylee ran the length of the barn, peering into each stall. "Bandit's not here!" she shouted. "Maybe we should search the grounds for—"

I heard heavy footsteps, but I couldn't warn Kaylee fast enough.

"Hey! What are you kids doing in here?"

I squinted toward the stable door and saw the black outline of a giant. The man must have stood seven feet tall and weighed 300 pounds—about the size of Maine. His hands went to his hips. I imagined six-shooters in holsters.

I watched, speechless, as the giant charged up the stallway, straight at us.

$\mathcal{K}$aylee," I whispered, "make a run for—"

But Kaylee barged past me and ran up the stallway, charging the giant. "Where's that buck-skin?" she demanded. "What have you done with him?"

The giant stopped. "You again?"

Kaylee marched all the way up to him. In the light, he might not have been a giant. But he was big. One look at his nose and I knew we were facing Lazy Lenny. I moved in beside Kaylee, figuring two were better than one. Plus, believe it or not, Leonard looked a little afraid of Kaylee.

Leonard hitched up his jeans, which would have made a perfect tent for the state of Rhode

Island. Then he turned and glared at me. "If you got money for a ride, pay up. If you ain't, go home."

"We're not going anywhere until I see Bandit!" Kaylee declared.

"Bandit?" he asked.

"The buckskin!" Kaylee shouted.

Leonard stormed down the stallway, with Kaylee at his heels. "He's in the last stall. You want to ride him or not?" He sounded like his vote was not.

"This is the horse you pawned off on me this morning. This is not Buckskin Bandit!" Kaylee insisted.

I peered into the last stall. "This isn't even a buckskin," I said, hating the sound of my voice. I always sound a little hoarse, with a raspy voice Lizzy claims she wishes she had. But I think I just sound hoarse. And the more nervous I get, the worse it sounds.

I cleared my throat and went on. "A true buckskin wouldn't have this much pigment in the hairs. Duns are duller colored than buckskins. See? This one has the dun factor, dark brown or black on the back and shoulder stripes, besides dark mane, tail, and legs."

"Whatever," the man said. "You want to ride or what?"

"Tell me where that horse is or I'm calling the ASPCA!" Kaylee roared.

I'd never seen this side of her. I liked it.

Leonard wiped his nose with the back of his hand. "That's it. Happy Trails is closed!"

Kaylee and I tried arguing, but the guy shooed us out of the stable and locked the door.

Nickers and I gave Kaylee a ride back to Summer's.

"Try not to worry about Bandit, Kaylee," I told her, as she slid off Nickers' rump at Stable-Mart. "Those pastures are so overgrown, Leonard could hide a herd of elephants on the property."

"I'll call the authorities tonight, Winnie. I've got the name—American Society for the Prevention of Cruelty to Animals. They'll have to send somebody out there."

Dad was waiting for me at home. I got a lecture on priorities and an inventor's single-mindedness. He didn't want to hear about Kaylee and Bandit and Happy Trails. We invented the rest of the night, until I fell asleep with a power drill in my hands. Then even Dad had to admit it was time to go to bed.

Sunday morning was gray, with the threat of rain. I slept in as long as possible, skipping Lizzy's peanut-butter pancakes and barely getting dressed before the Barker Bus came by for us.

The Barker Bus is really a yellow van, big enough to hold a big family, including the Barker dogs, Dad, Lizzy, and me. The dogs hadn't come to church with us, so their little seat belts, invented by my dad, hung empty on the floor.

"Thanks for the ride, Mrs. Barker," I said as Dad, Lizzy, and I climbed over the Barker brothers.

Mrs. Barker turned around from the driver's seat. "Anytime."

We exchanged hi's with everybody, except Granny Barker, who had stayed home with a cold. Dad fastened his seat belt, then turned to talk to Mr. Barker, who was wedged in the far backseat between Johnny and Luke. Mr. Barker used to play football at Ashland University. And even though now he's kind of this poet professor, he looks like he could still play football for them.

"How's the invention business?" Barker asked.

"Don't get Dad started," I whispered.

Mark, age seven, and two-year-old William were fussing over who got to sit next to Lizzy. My sister settled the feud by moving Mark and sitting between the boys.

"So does anybody know who's taking Ralph's place this morning?" Lizzy asked, as Mrs. Barker turned the van around.

"Where's Ralph?" Barker asked.

"Wedding. In Michigan, I think," I answered.

We filed into church and took our spots in the Barker pew across the aisle from Pat. As usual, Catman and M made their entrance just as the organ started playing. M's in eighth grade with Catman. As usual, M was dressed totally in black. He's a pretty good friend of mine, even though I still don't know what the *M* stands for. I don't think anybody does, even Catman.

When it was time for the sermon, Mr. Barker walked to the front of the church. "I've never given a sermon before," he began.

I glanced over at Barker, who looked as surprised as I was. Mrs. Barker was grinning, though.

"I better warn you that my students think I lecture too long," Mr. Barker continued. "But I'll try not to commit that sin here."

We laughed. I was nervous for him, but he sounded like a natural pastor.

"When Ralph asked me to stand in for him, I had no idea what I'd say. But I finally decided to talk about joy. Being happy. Hey, who can get on my case for that, right?

"Tom Blake, a colleague at AU, was awarded a grant by the university last week. I was truly happy for Tom—" he paused and wrinkled his forehead—"until I started wondering, Why didn't I get that grant? And you know what? For the rest of the week, even though I knew Tom deserved that grant, every time I saw him, I felt rotten inside."

I liked Mr. Barker's stories, but the last couple of nights with so little sleep started catching up with me. I yawned, then tried to hide it by covering my mouth.

"Last Tuesday," he continued, "I ran into an old high school buddy I hadn't seen in 20 years. He'd lost 40 pounds and looked better than he did in high school. 'Way to go!' I told him. But you know, I wasn't all that happy for him if you want to know the honest truth. Why?" He patted his stomach. We chuckled.

I closed my eyes. I couldn't imagine being so old that I hadn't seen somebody in 20 years.

Mr. Barker's voice was low, like a bass drum. It made me want to drift off to sleep. With my eyes closed, I tried to listen.

"Ever watch a buddy hit a home run, but you strike out?" Mr. Barker asked us. "How did you feel? Real happy? Your buddy's full of joy, right? Are you? See, what God's been teaching me is that there's a lot of joy in the world. But it may not all start and end in my backyard. I might have to be happy for someone else."

I could have dozed off for the ending. When I opened my eyes, Catman and M had written their initials all over my bulletin.

On the ride home, the Barker boys gave their dad a hard time about keeping his sermon-giving a secret. Dad, Lizzy, and I kept telling him what a good job he did.

Kaylee was sitting on our front step when the Barker Bus pulled to our curb. "I didn't know where else to go," she said. "I didn't sleep all night, worrying about Bandit. I left a message at the ASPCA, but who knows when they'll send somebody to investigate."

Suddenly thunder boomed, and the skies opened. We hurried inside as rain poured down in sheets.

"Sweet!" Lizzy exclaimed, taking Kaylee's jacket. "Looks like you'll have to stay for dinner."

We didn't get a chance to talk about Happy Trails over dinner because Dad wouldn't stop talking about the Magnificent Multishower. But as soon as we finished our pistachio pudding, I hustled Kaylee out to the barn. She fussed over Buddy, and she even liked Annie Goat. We went around in circles, though, trying to figure out how we could make Leonard tell us what he'd done with Bandit.

Dad and I drove Kaylee home in our cattle truck when the rain let up. We bounced up the curved driveway and squealed to a stop in front of her house. Before I knew Kaylee lived there, I'd passed the Hsu three-story, brick house dozens of times. And each time I'd wondered why anybody who could afford a home like that would live in a small town like Ashland.

Both Mr. and Mrs. Hsu stepped out to greet their daughter. They must have been shocked to see her climb out of a cattle truck, but they didn't let on. Instead they walked up to the truck and introduced themselves to Dad.

Dad and I drove back home. And in honor of Sunday, he only made us work on the shower until a little after 10. Then I remembered the invention outline was due in the morning. It took me another two hours to write it up.

Monday morning I raced to first period and slid
into my seat as the bell rang.

Barker was already at his desk next to mine.
"Made it," he whispered.

Ms. Brumby, our English teacher, was dressed
as spring. Her silky shirt was the green of an oak
tree in May. Her skirt, jacket, scarf, and shoes
were light green, like spring buds on a poplar.

I still can't look at our English teacher without
thinking of a real Brumby—the bony, Roman-
nosed, Australian scrub horse that most people
have given up on training.

I watched Ms. Brumby write on the chalkboard in perfect block letters: *Title, Introduction,
Thesis, How-to paragraphs, Conclusion*. I felt an
essay—or even worse, a speech—coming on.

Kaylee, in the back row, was wearing khakis
and a short-sleeved, red sweater that made her
shiny hair look even darker. She whispered
something to me, but I couldn't understand.
Summer and her herd were making too much
noise.

"What did you say?" I whispered back.

"Winifred? Is there something you'd like to share with the class?" Ms. Brumby roared.

I faced front. "Um . . . no, ma'am."

Behind me, I heard Summer's annoying laugh, followed by the giggles of her followers.

"Then let's begin." Ms. Brumby's spring green high heels clicked when she crossed to the stuff she'd written on the board. You would have thought the words had been typed by a giant typewriter. "These are the parts of the speech you will prepare for your science-fair projects."

Speech? I raised my hand for probably the third time all year in this class.

Ms. Brumby nodded at me. The toe of her pointy green shoe tapped, as if to hurry me.

"Do we—" I cleared my throat—"I mean . . . a speech? I thought we just had to do an invention for extra credit."

"Well, you do have to prepare a speech, regardless of your participation in the science fair." She smiled at the rest of the class. "For those of you who will be showing your projects, you will be asked by the judges to explain your invention." She tapped the board. "This is how you will answer."

My most hated thing in all of school is giving

a speech. I get so nervous, my voice sounds like geese honking.

Even my inventor dad couldn't help me with this one.

$\mathcal{P}$at Haven was shuffling through her desk drawer when Kaylee and I walked in. We only had a minute, but we told her about going to Happy Trails and getting run off by Leonard.

"You girls listen here. Stay clear of Lazy Lenny. I mean it. I'll look in on Mrs. Pulaski and see what I can find out. Don't you worry."

The bell had rung, and kids were throwing paper wads and pencils.

Kaylee and I took our seats. It makes me mad when kids in Pat's class are obnoxious and loud just because they know how nice Pat is.

It took a couple of minutes for her to get everybody's attention. "Let's hear about some of these grand inventions. Barker, you lead off."

Barker did a great job explaining his dog

greeting cards, even though he couldn't have had time to write a real speech already. He showed us one card, made out of rawhide chews, with Slim Jim beef jerky spelling out *Happy birthday to my best friend!*

Other kids had pretty cool inventions too. Sal stood up. She and I had become friends when I gentled her Miniature Falabella, Amigo. Sal was wearing hoop earrings the size of Virginia and West Virginia. "This is so tight, you guys! I'm inventing earrings—"

"Hey, there's an original idea," Brian interrupted.

Sal hit him over the head with her notebook. "Earrings that are also earplugs! Like in case someone, like Brian, is talking, and you want to shut him out."

We applauded, and Sal sat down.

Grant Baines had a great invention. Back when school started in the fall, I'd worked with his horse, Eager Star. Since then, he'd won a dozen barrel races with his horse. Grant held up a battered can of grape soda and a straw as long as his forearm.

"My invention shirt has a pocket right here." He pointed to the spot where he'd have to put his hand if we said the Pledge of Allegiance to the flag. "The can fits in here. And with this straw, I can drink on the go. Look, Mom, no hands!" He pretended to swing a bat while sipping from his straw.

Almost everybody had something, although some of the inventions were kind of dumb, as if they'd just been thought up on the spot. Like a three-headed pen, or a notebook that opens from either side, or fake eyes so you look awake when you fall asleep in class.

Kaylee had a great idea. She was inventing a perfume using only spring wildflowers and grasses.

I was glad Pat didn't call on me.

"Summer? Why don't you share your idea?" Pat asked.

Summer glanced around the room, her gaze resting on me. "I don't know," she said, like she wanted us to beg. "If anybody copied my idea, I'd refuse to have another idea so long as I live."

Note to self: Seriously consider copying Summer's idea, whatever it is.

"I don't think we have to worry about that, Summer," Pat said.

Summer ran her fingers through her long,

blonde hair. Her fingertips didn't even slow down. I don't think my fingers could have made it through my wavy hair.

"Oh, all right," Summer conceded, as if we'd begged and begged. "We all know how women rely on finger-combing their hair throughout the day." She shook her hair, as if she were filming a shampoo commercial. "But fingers alone can't always do the job. What's a woman to do?"

She smiled around the room, especially at all the guys. "So I've invented tiny combs and brushes that fit on my fingertips. I can carry them in my purse."

Girls *ooh*ed and *ah*ed. Even I had to admit it was a great idea, not that I'd ever buy one. But girls like Summer would love it. And there are a lot more girls like Summer than there are girls like me.

When the bell rang, Kaylee and I walked out together. We battled the stampede to the cafeteria and sat at my usual table, which was totally empty.

Kaylee bit into her egg-salad sandwich and opened her chips. "So what did you think of the other inventions?"

"I hate to admit it, but Summer's sounded pretty good," I said.

"I wonder if she knows they sell finger-combs in Japan." She poured from her thermos and took a drink. "My parents and I saw them when we traveled to Japan last summer."

Japan? Lizzy and I hadn't been out of Ohio since we'd moved to Ashland.

We were quiet for a couple of minutes, eating our sandwiches. I said grace without making a big deal of it. *Thanks for my lunch, God. And I really don't think it's fair that Summer Spidell is inventing something Japanese people already have. Plus, could I go to Japan someday? or at least Pennsylvania? Amen.*

Catman and M sat across from us and lined up their hot-lunch trays. Each tray held six peanut-butter sandwiches, no jelly. Catman grinned hello, and M raised an eyebrow at Kaylee and me, one each.

"Hey to you guys too," I said.

Catman's blond hair hung straight to his shoulders, but M's long, black hair was pulled back in a ponytail. When I started at Ashland Middle School, I was kind of afraid of M, which was pretty dumb. He is definitely one of the good guys.

It was funny to watch M and Catman nibble the crusts off their sandwiches as if they were mice, racing.

"Anyway," I said, turning back to Kaylee, "I've been thinking a lot about Happy Trails. We need to go back there after school and search for Bandit. That buckskin has to be hidden in one of those back pastures."

"You heard what Pat said about Leonard, Winnie. He's not going to let us wander around looking for a horse he claims doesn't even exist."

"Bummer," Catman muttered.

Kaylee bit into her apple. "I know Bandit's there. Leonard claimed those other horses didn't exist either. Remember? He said he only had five horses . . . until he needed two more. The only reason he brought those horses out was so he could collect money from all seven riders."

"That's it!" I exclaimed. "We'll do the same thing! We'll show up with eight riders. No way he'll turn down the extra money! He'll have to use Bandit!"

"Winnie, that's a great idea!" Kaylee's smile faded. "But where are we going to get eight riders?"

I was already thinking about that. "Okay. You

and me, that's two. Lizzy's out." Dad might have done it, but it would be hard enough to talk him into letting me have an hour away from the workshop. "Let's ask Sal and Hawk!"

Summer's table was just behind ours. I shouted over at them, "Hawk! Sal! Come here a minute!"

Hawk got up, and Summer grabbed her arm and said something, laughing. But Hawk didn't laugh along. Instead she came over and sat across from me, next to Catman. "I am glad for the chance to talk with you, Winnie. I was thinking. Your birthday is coming up, right?"

"Winnie," Kaylee said, "you never told me. When's your birthday?"

"March 24th," Hawk answered. "I was thinking it might be fun to have a horse birthday party Saturday, where those of us who have horses bring them."

"What a great idea!" Kaylee exclaimed.

Something inside me felt heavy. "I don't do much for birthdays, Hawk. But thanks."

"I would do all the organizing and—," Hawk began.

"Look! Here's Sal!" I said, cutting her off. I knew Hawk meant well, and I was grateful. But

I'd told her about my mom's accident. She should have understood.

Sal slid in next to M. "What's up?" I hadn't noticed before that she had a couple of new purple stripes in her red hair.

Catman and M just kept munching sandwiches.

"We need your help," I started. "We need to get eight people together for a trail ride."

"Hello? Unless Amigo grew overnight, he's still too little to ride," Sal said.

"I think a trail ride sounds like fun," Hawk said. "I have not ridden Towaco for a week."

"Well, that's the thing," Kaylee said. "We need you to ride one of the horses at Happy Trails."

"Happy Trails?" Sal's face looked like she'd swallowed lemons. "That dump? I'd never let Amigo play with those horses—definitely wrong side of the tracks."

"It's important, Sal." I glanced at Kaylee and got a go-ahead nod. "We think they're mistreating one of their horses, maybe more. We need to see all eight horses, so we have to have eight riders."

"Man, that burns me!" Sal reached over and ate one of M's pickles. He raised his eyebrow at her. "Count me in!"

"The same for me," Hawk said.

"Great!" I couldn't believe it was this easy. Four down. Four to go. "We'll meet right after school and go—"

"After school?" Hawk asked. "I can't do it right after school."

"Why not?" Kaylee asked.

Hawk stared at her fingernails and shifted in her seat, stealing a glance up at Catman. "I . . . I told Mother I would do something after school."

"Hawk!" I cried. "Can't you tell your mom you'll do it tomorrow?"

Hawk shook her head.

"So what's so important?" Sal asked.

Hawk took a deep breath. "I have a job. A modeling job." She almost swallowed the last words.

"Victoria, that's so tight!" Sal shouted. She turned around to Summer's table. "Hey, you guys! Did you know Vic here got herself a modeling job?"

Summer wheeled around, frowning. "Where?"

Hawk turned sheepishly. "It is no big deal. Really. Ford Models. It is all Mother's idea."

Summer dropped her spoon.

"Hey, isn't that where you applied over Christmas vacation, Summer?" Sal asked. "Ford Models? Yeah, that was it, right?"

"I don't remember," Summer lied. You could tell by the way she wouldn't look at Hawk.

"You are so lucky!" Kristine, another girl in our class, exclaimed. "And they pay for taking your picture?"

Kristine is pretty smart. I had to think she knew the answer to that one. I wondered if she'd asked it just to make Summer even more miserable.

"I will not model regularly," Hawk explained. "Only for special jobs."

"Special jobs, huh?" Grant repeated. "Sounds great, Victoria. Way to go!"

"Yeah, Hawk. Congratulations." I tried to mean it. Hawk is probably my best friend. I wanted to be happy for her. I was, really. It's just that I knew nobody would ever pay money to take a picture of me. And I was the one who could have used that extra money. Hawk has two divorced parents who try to outdo each other by shoving money at her.

"I am really sorry," Hawk said, getting up from the table. "Is the stable open in the evening? I should be finished by five o'clock. Mother could drop me off at Happy Trails."

"They're open until eight on Mondays," Kaylee said. "Let's do it!"

"Works for me," I said. "Gives me a little time for Dad and the invention."

"I'm in. Call me, though, and remind me," Sal said, following Hawk back to Summer's table.

As soon as Hawk rejoined the popular group, she was showered with a million questions about modeling. I watched silent Summer and imagined steam coming out of her ears. If envy really is green, then Summer was a match for Ms. Brumby's color of the day.

"Well, we've got Sal and Hawk," I said, throwing the rest of my lunch back into the sack.

"But where are we going to get four more riders by five o'clock?" Kaylee sounded desperate.

Without looking like I was praying, I asked God in my head, *Would you please find us four more riders?*

M cleared his throat. He kept clearing it until we looked at him. He was holding up a half-eaten sandwich, nibbled in the shape of a perfect *U*. Next to him, Catman held up one of his sandwiches, nibbled into a less-than-perfect but clearly readable *S*.

"U.S.?" Kaylee asked. "As in the United States?"

I stared at the sandwiches. If they'd wanted periods after the letters, I knew they would have nibbled them there. "It's *us*, right?"

Catman grinned. I think M's nose twitched.

"*Us*, as in you?" I asked. "Would you guys go with us to Happy Trails?"

"Sounds groovy!" Catman answered. "We thought you'd never ask."

"That's so nice of you!" Kaylee agreed. "But we still need two more riders."

M and Catman each grabbed a different sandwich and held it up. They'd eaten the sandwiches, leaving only the outlines of the letters *C* and *B*.

"*CB?*" Kaylee asked. "Like truckers use? Ask truckers, over a CB?"

But I was looking at the tiny bread dots next to each letter. *C.* and *B.* Initials. "Claire and Bart!" I shouted. Claire and Bart Coolidge are Catman's parents. He calls them by their first names when they're not around.

Catman and M grinned, finished their sandwiches in one bite, and rose from the table.

"Catman, are you sure your parents will want to ride with us?" I asked.

"It's cool," Catman assured us. "My pad. Five o'clock."

After school, I biked straight to my barn to say hey to Nickers, Buddy, Towaco, and Annie Goat. It would have been great to take Nickers for a long ride, but I knew better.

Dad was waiting for me when I stepped into the house. "Where have you been? We have work to do, Winnie! Two of the showerheads aren't working. We need more caulking. . . ." He kept up a steady stream of inventor talk as I followed him to the workshop.

"Off to invent?" Lizzy asked when we passed through the kitchen. She was dumping stuff from cans into a casserole dish.

I waved at her as we flew by, but I don't think Dad heard her.

"I should have dinner ready by four," Lizzy

called after us. In our house we eat when it's ready or when we're ready, anytime between three and nine.

For the next hour Dad and I sanded and caulked and talked. We just talked about the science fair, but it was still talk. In the past couple of days, Dad and I had said more words to each other than we had in the past couple of months.

Lizzy stuck her head into the shop to tell us dinner was ready.

"Thanks, Lizzy. I'll have to eat fast. I promised Catman I'd be at his house at five." I started to go in.

"Just bring Winnie and me a plate out here, will you, Lizzy?" Dad asked from inside the shower stall. His voice sounded like a cartoon character. "We need to work right through dinner."

Lizzy brought us plates of food, and I scarfed down the casserole without recognizing the taste. But it was crunchy and good and peanut buttery.

"Thanks, Lizzy," I said, handing her my empty plate. "Dad, I have to go."

Dad glanced at his pocket watch. "It won't take you twenty minutes to walk to Catman's. We can still fix that one showerhead."

"But I have to muck stalls before I go."

"Lizzy will do it. Won't you, honey?" Dad said it so it didn't really sound like a question.

"Really?" I turned to Lizzy. It would be great if she did it for me. It would only take me two minutes to grain the horses. I wouldn't even be late to Catman's.

Lizzy hesitated. "I was going to meet Geri at the creek."

"You can still do that. We must all sacrifice for invention!" Dad dove to the ground and lifted the shower stall. "There! Winnie, grab that screw."

And we were back at it.

I had to run down the stallway to dump grain in the horses' bins before racing to Catman's. Lizzy was dodging Annie Goat and throwing manure into the wheelbarrow. Her shovelfuls were so small, it would take her as long to muck one stall as it took me to do the whole barn.

Lizzy looked up from her shovel as I was

dashing out of the barn. "Winnie, are you and Catman going out to get parts for your invention?"

"Nope," I hollered back. "Trail riding!"

"What? But that's not—"

"Thanks for doing the stalls, Lizzy!" I shouted as I tore out of the barn.

I ran all the way to Coolidge Castle, my name for Catman's three-story house that looks haunted from the outside but like a 100-year-old palace inside.

Everybody was already loading into a long black limo that Mr. Coolidge must have driven home for the occasion. He owns Smart Bart's Used Cars and can drive any vehicle on the lot whenever he wants to.

About a dozen cats swarmed the car. I recognized Gorham, Griffin, Hancock, and Hanson, four cats from Wilhemina's litter. Catman had named them all after first presidents, guys in our country's history who had the job before the real presidency kicked in for George Washington.

Catman should be a history teacher when he grows up. All he'd have to do is take his cats to class and explain their names. Wilhemina, for example, the fat orange cat who tried to climb into the limo with me, was named after the author Charles Dickens' cat. Or Rice, the white cat named after David Rice Atchinson, who was a U.S. president for a day.

"Sorry I'm late!" I said, climbing into the seat between M and Sal. I couldn't believe Sal beat me here.

Two long seats, which could have doubled as couches, faced each other across thick gray carpet. Sal, M, and I fit easily into one seat, with Catman and his mom across from us. Behind me, the glass pane to the front seat rolled down, and Mr. Coolidge handed me a tall, frosty glass of limeade. Everyone in the car had one, complete with a slice of lemon, an umbrella, and a tiny leaf floating on top.

"Hey, Winnie!" Bart Coolidge greeted me from the driver's seat, with a tip of his 10-gallon hat. His hairpiece slid forward, but it went back in place when he put his hat back on. I don't know where he'd found it, but around his neck was a Tweety Bird tie. Not the Tweety tie he usually wore, but a new one. Each yellow bird wore a 10-gallon hat. "I'm rearing to ride!" he exclaimed.

"It is so good to see you!" Claire Coolidge declared. She leaned across to fluff up my hair.

"Such gorgeous waves!" She's the only one who feels this way about my hair. It's funny, because she runs Claire's Beauty Salon on Main Street, so you'd think she'd have better taste in hair. Mr. and Mrs. Coolidge were wearing matching cowboy outfits, complete with boots, hats, black jeans, and white yoked shirts that snapped down the front.

"Don't you love Winnie's hair, Sal?" Mrs. Coolidge asked.

Sal eyed my hair, which was only halfway in the ponytail it had started out in. "I guess," she said, not sounding convinced. "Get this, Winnie. Claire's been doing my hair for over a year, and I didn't even know she was Catman's mom."

"Next time you're by the salon, Winnie, I'd love to stripe your hair the way I do Sal's!" Claire offered.

Note to self: Do not go near Claire's Beauty Salon.

"Summer used to get her hair done at Claire's too," Sal commented, "until she started going to this stylist in Cleveland."

Mrs. Coolidge frowned. "Summer. Summer. Ah yes. Now I remember. Long, rather wimpy, limp, blonde hair. Needed a lot of help with conditioner and gels, as I recall."

I really like Mrs. Coolidge.

"Sa-a-ay!" Mr. Coolidge wrenched his short, round body around the steering wheel so he could face us. "I'll deny it if you pass this piece of information to anyone down at Smart Bart's Used Cars, but I miss the days of good, old-fashioned horseback riding."

"So you've ridden before, Mr. Coolidge?" I asked, relieved.

"Have I ridden?" He looked offended. "Why, in my day they called me Cowboy Bart! I could make those ponies circle. Cameras flashed when I rode by."

"That's great," I said. "How about you, Mrs. Coolidge?"

"I did take a buggy ride in Central Park once. But I don't believe I have ever seen the world from the back of a horse. Mr. Coolidge says it's like driving a car, though."

That made me nervous. Mrs. Coolidge had been trying to get her driver's license ever since I'd known her. I'd have to be sure she and Sal got the gentlest horses.

"The lovely Mrs. Coolidge is a natural at everything she undertakes," her husband proclaimed.

"Now Mr. Coolidge," said his wife.

Catman and M hadn't spoken, at least not out loud. But I had a feeling they were saying volumes to each other, exchanging expressions at racehorse speed.

Mr. Coolidge revved the engine and shot down the bumpy driveway. "Sa-a-ay!" he shouted back. "What did the driverless car say to his friend, the bat?"

I started cracking up.

"Why are you laughing?" Sal whispered.

"You'll see," I whispered back. Mr. Coolidge has so many corny jokes. All he has to do is start one, and I lose it. "I give," I replied. "What did the driverless car say to the bat?"

"'You drive me, Batty!' Get it? 'You drive me batty!' " He laughed in windy huffs that made me think of horses' snorting. "I've got a million of 'em!"

Sal cracked up too, shaking her head.

Mr. Coolidge tried out half a dozen equally corny jokes on us as he drove to Happy Trails. Most had something to do with horsepower. By the time we got there, Sal was laughing so hard her mascara was running in streams down the sides of her face.

Hawk and Kaylee were already at the stable when we drove up. They came running to the car and grabbed me the second I opened the door.

"I told him our friends were meeting us here, and we'd need all eight horses," Kaylee whispered.

"And," Hawk continued, "that man insisted they only have seven horses."

"Then—" Kaylee took over again—"that old woman, the one who yelled at us before, poked her head out of her house and asked what all the arguing was about."

"The large man's face turned white," Hawk said. "He was definitely frightened of her. You should have seen Kaylee. She told the old woman that we had wanted our party of eight to ride together. But since Happy Trails only had seven horses, none of us would be riding."

"Way to go, Kaylee!" I wished I could have been there to see it.

Kaylee picked up the story. "Then Leonard said it had all been a mistake, and of course they had eight horses for us. So he walked out to the pasture and hasn't been back since. The woman went back inside her house, but we're still waiting for Leonard to bring the eighth horse. It's got to be Bandit."

"You did it!" I couldn't believe our plan was actually working.

Kaylee and I made our way to the barn, while Hawk stayed outside to greet the other riders. We found the seven horses saddled and bridled, waiting in their stalls.

From behind the barn came a squeal, followed by a smack. Then Leonard plodded into the barn through the back door. Bandit, ears flat back, walked stiffly behind him.

I had a good idea of what Leonard had been doing to the horse—from the squeal, the smack, the look of terror and anger in Bandit's eyes.

It made me want to grow three feet taller and 200 pounds heavier and give Leonard a dose of his own medicine.

Chapter 11

Bandit's head jerked with every move Leonard made as they did a tug-of-war up the stallway. The buckskin's eyes were rimmed white, and his flanks quivered. He looked ready to bolt.

"I might have known you'd bring your little friend," Leonard grumbled.

Bandit slammed on his brakes, his forelegs stiff. He threw up his head.

"Get up here!" Leonard shouted, jerking the reins. "I'll show you who's boss!"

"Stop it!" Kaylee cried, running up to them.

"Maybe now you can see why I try to keep this horse away from the customers," Leonard said, pulling on Bandit's leadrope. "He's no good. I told the old woman we ought to get rid of him." He looped the rope around a stall post and pulled a broken-down saddle off the railing.

Bandit tugged against the rope.

"You stop that!" Leonard bellowed. He charged the gelding, then stopped, as if realizing he wasn't the only human in the barn.

"I'll saddle him," I offered. "Please?"

He frowned at Bandit, then at me. "Knock yourself out." He tossed me the saddle, almost knocking me out himself.

I set down the saddle and walked up to the quivering Bandit. I could see myself in his watery eyes. From outside the barn came Mr. Coolidge's voice as he told another joke, while Sal choked with laughter.

Kaylee moved up to Bandit's head and held out her hand.

Bandit's ears shot back.

"Careful, Kaylee," I warned.

She took her hand back. "Oh, Winnie. He's worse than before. What are we going to do?"

"I'll tell you what we're not going to do," I said, touching Bandit's neck lightly, then increasing the pressure to a scratch. "We're not going to ride him. Not like this."

"You're right," she agreed. "He's so scared, Winnie. I can't stand it."

One by one Leonard led the seven tired horses out of the barn. Each time he returned for another one, he smirked at us. With just the dun remaining, Leonard stopped in front of us. "So, couldn't even get that beast saddled, could you?"

"I changed my mind," I said. "I don't feel like riding."

"No refunds!" Leonard barked.

"That's okay," I said. "I'll just stay here until the rest of them get back."

"No way, Winnie!" Kaylee cried. "I'm staying with Bandit!"

"Well, whoever's coming better come," Leonard said, shoving Bandit into the nearest stall.

I tried to get Kaylee to go on the ride, but she refused to leave Bandit. Finally I gave up. "Okay. But don't go into the stall. Promise? Just stay here. Talk to Bandit. Laugh. Let him see what it's like when people are happy."

I joined the others outside. Hawk was helping Mrs. Coolidge onto a dirty Palomino. Then she moved over to Sal and gave her last-minute riding instructions.

Leonard led out the dun last and handed him to me.

"Outta sight!" Catman cried, sliding off the bay he was mounted on. "Swap, Winnie? That horse looks like a Siamese cat, man."

I'd never thought about it, but Catman had a point. The dun was cream-colored with brown shadings like a Siamese. "Be my guest," I said.

I held the dun while Catman mounted. Then I climbed into the stiff saddle on the bay. "Did this horse used to be a Trotter?" I asked Leonard. "A Standardbred?"

"Yeah." Leonard looked surprised. And suspicious. "How'd you know that?"

"Trade secret," I said. But it wasn't that hard. The horse was powerfully built, without the refined look of a Thoroughbred. His body was long, with sloping shoulders and short legs.

I glanced around at the horses the others had ended up with. All the horses seemed so tuckered out that I didn't think we'd have much trouble with them on the trail.

"Tallyho!" cried Mr. Coolidge.

Leonard pointed to the trail and told us to ride out and back. At least that was one good thing. None of the horses had to carry him.

"Them horses could do the route blindfolded," he said, getting into his battered pickup. "I'll be back before you are."

"Hawk, you lead!" I hollered as she mounted a sorrel mare. "I'll bring up the rear."

The horses lined themselves up as they plodded on the rough trail toward thick trees. Mrs. Coolidge pulled her horse out of second in line and let Sal go in front of her. She said she wanted to be in front of her husband. Mr. Coolidge's hat was crooked, and I hoped his toupee would stay on. He leaned to the side, but I didn't want to insult him by telling him to sit up straighter.

For the first 15 minutes, Hawk couldn't get her horse to move faster than a painfully slow walk. I had to keep pulling up the Trotter so he wouldn't trot into the back of M's horse, who would then ram into Catman's horse.

Sal, who had moved in behind Hawk, kept a steady conversation going with her. After a while, Sal turned back and shouted, "Hey! You're all invited to Winnie's barn for a horse birthday party Saturday morning! Amigo will love it! M, you can hang with Buddy. Catman, we know you'll bring cats."

"Sal, I—" But I didn't know what to say. I still hated birthdays—my birthday anyway. I'd vowed I'd never celebrate March 24th again. Too many pictures stored up in my head.

But some of the older pictures were good ones. A photo shot to my brain. I must have been about eight because Lizzy and I were almost the same height. Mom was holding Buttermilk, her buckskin, so I could ride her. I was wearing new boots I'd gotten for my birthday. But the real gift was Mom trusting me with her horse.

"So aren't you going to say anything, Winnie?" Sal was twisted around in her saddle—one hand on her horse's rump, the other clutching the saddle horn. "We're bringing the cake and everything—unless Lizzy insists on baking it. Hint, hint."

I looked up to the front of the line. Hawk was staring back at me. Our eyes held each other's. And I knew. It wasn't that she had forgotten how I felt about birthdays. Hawk understood. She just wanted to kick me past it.

"A horse birthday party, huh?" I said slowly. When I looked at it like I was somebody else, somebody whose mother hadn't died like mine had, it was just about the nicest thing anybody had wanted to do for me in a long time. "I like it."

"That's better." Sal turned back around.

Ahead of me, Catman was staring at something, holding it up to the sinking sun.

"What have you got, Catman?" I hollered.

He waved what looked like a tiny leaf he must have pulled from a tree.

M grabbed a leaf from a tree as we passed by. He held it up, exactly like Catman.

I plucked a leaf off the next tree and stared at it, holding it up to the sun. It was green and nice and everything, but nothing special. "I don't get it!" I shouted.

But M did. "Blocks out the sun," he explained. "Decidedly amazing."

I looked at the leaf again. M was right. As we rocked along on our horses, I stared at the leaf and couldn't see the sun behind it. Amazing that something that small could block out something so big.

"Mrs. Coolidge?" Mr. Coolidge's panicky voice startled me. "Darling, where are you going?"

"I'm not doing it!" she hollered back, terror in her voice.

I dropped my leaf and saw that Mrs. Coolidge's horse was very slowly walking past Sal's horse, reclaiming her rightful spot as second in line.

Mr. Coolidge yelled, "Stop that horse! It's running away with my wife!"

"No, it's not, Mr. Coolidge!" I shouted up. "The horses are used to taking the trail in a certain order. She'll be fine when she's back in the right slot."

But he wasn't listening to me. "Mrs. Coolidge!" he cried. "Hang on! I'm coming!" He gripped the saddle horn. "Yeee-haw!"

I'm not sure what he did next. But suddenly his horse sprang to life. The mare gave a little buck I could have sworn she didn't have in her and broke out of line in a trot.

"Pull back on the reins!" I yelled as loud as I could.

But he was only holding the tips of the reins. So when he pulled, nothing happened. In fact, the mare trotted faster, past Sal, past Mrs. Coolidge, past Hawk.

"Stop!" cried Mr. Coolidge.

But the mare had a taste of the lead and wasn't about to give it up. She broke to a canter, sending Mr. Coolidge farther sideways. His legs stuck out. One hand continued to grip the saddle horn, and the other clutched his hat as his horse took off through the woods in a real, live runaway.

Go, Bart!" Catman shouted as his dad's horse disappeared into the forest ahead of us.

I couldn't believe Mr. Coolidge's mount had that much spunk. I knew the horse would just run back to the barn, but I was afraid Mr. Coolidge might fall off first.

"Come on, Trotter!" I coaxed, urging my bay out of line.

Catman started to follow me, but then M's horse pulled out to follow him.

"Stay in line, Catman! Please!" I cried. "I'll get your dad!"

"Save Mr. Coolidge!" his wife pleaded, as my Trotter broke to a fast trot.

"Don't worry!" I yelled back. I wished I didn't have the stupid saddle between the Trotter and me. He wasn't reading my leg cues to canter. But he trotted faster and faster as I guided him toward the cloud of dust ahead of us.

When I spotted the tail of Mr. Coolidge's mount, I leaned forward on Trotter's neck. He trotted even faster, threatening to bounce his saddle off. But the gap narrowed between Mr. Coolidge and us. I could see the Tweety Bird tie flapping in the wind.

"Hang on, Mr. Coolidge!" I screamed.

My horse easily overtook the loping runaway. Without slowing down, I leaned over and grabbed the reins. "Whoa!"

His horse slowed to a trot, then to a walk. Then she stopped.

"Are you all right, Mr. Coolidge?" His toupee and hat were gone, and his face was beaded in sweat.

"I was less than forthcoming," he said, panting, "in recounting my equestrian exploits. I did ride several times, but only as a young lad. Ponies. At the circus . . . in a circle. A couple of times I sat on a horse to have my picture taken."

"That's okay, Mr. Coolidge." I spotted his hat a few yards away. "You thought you were saving your wife. That was very brave." I hopped off

Trotter and recovered the crumpled, 10-gallon hat. I pretended not to notice the toupee inside as I handed the hat over to Mr. Coolidge.

He plunked both hat and toupee onto his bald head, straightened his Tweety Bird tie, and picked up his horse's reins. "Shall we go?"

We joined the others and finished our ride without incident.

Back at Happy Trails, we piled into the limo. I waited until we reached the end of the drive before tapping on the chauffeur window. Mr. Coolidge stopped the car and rolled down the window.

"Mr. Coolidge, would you mind if Kaylee and I walked back?" I asked.

"That's exactly what I was thinking!" Kaylee said.

"Are you crazy?" Sal asked. "It's two miles to your house."

"Winnie, won't your dad be waiting for you?" Hawk asked.

Hawk was right. But I'd deal with that when I got home. For now, Bandit was my main worry.

As soon as the limo drove off, Kaylee and I sneaked back to the barn. The sky was a deep smoky gray, throwing jagged shadows on the ground. Leonard already had the horses unsaddled. He hadn't even bothered to cool them down or groom them. It was all I could do not to barge in there and take care of the horses myself.

But I had Bandit to think about.

We lurked outside the barn until Leonard finished stabling the other horses. When they were all stashed in stalls, he barged into Bandit's stall. I hated the way he manhandled Bandit, jerking the buckskin through the back of the barn.

Kaylee and I ducked from tree to tree, following, as Leonard dragged Bandit through pasture after pasture. We stayed back as far as we could without losing them. Finally he stopped at a scrappy pasture surrounded by hedge-apple trees and filled with thorny bushes. Then he shoved Bandit through the gate and smacked him on the rump. Bandit took off at a dead gallop.

We waited until we were sure Leonard was gone. Then we walked up to the splintered fence topped with rusty barbed wire.

"Here, Bandit!" Kaylee called.

Bandit raced around the pasture three times and stopped as far away from us as he could get. Kaylee picked grass and held it over the fence. We both tried calling him, but he wouldn't budge. All the fight had gone out of him, but so had the life. He twitched in the middle of the pasture, his tail between his legs.

"Isn't there anything we can do?" Kaylee asked.

I tried to think like Mom. She would have wanted Bandit to get a vision for the kind of world, the kind of herd he could be part of if he chose to join up. I thought of Mom's buckskin and tried to think of everything she'd done to win over that horse.

Then I remembered. "Sing," I murmured.

"Did you say, 'sing'?" Kaylee stared at me like I had a nose worthy of honking.

I nodded. "We have to make Bandit want to join us, to become part of our herd. Bandit has to see how happy we are, Kaylee. Then he'll want a piece of that happiness."

I wished Mom could be here to explain it better. I wanted Kaylee to understand. "See, when something bad happens to a horse, it's always right there with him. Like no matter what human he looks at, there's that bad thing somebody did to him. We have to change the way Bandit sees the world."

Kaylee smiled over at me. Then she started singing, "'Camptown ladies sing this song. Doo-da, doo-da!'" She whispered, as if afraid Bandit would overhear, "I can't think of any other horse songs."

I joined her, faking the words when I couldn't remember them. "'Camptown racetrack's two miles long. Oh, doo-da day!'" We sang a dozen choruses, as woodpeckers pecked, robins chirped, and the pasture scent of clover and bittersweet mixed with the smell of sweat and horse.

Later, as we walked back across the fields in moonlight, we had to admit that Bandit hadn't shown any signs of appreciating our singing. But at least now we had a place to see him and a plan to draw him into our world.

When I finally got home from Happy Trails, Lizzy was waiting for me. "Where have you been, Winnie? Dad's been going crazy! And I was so worried!"

"Take it easy, Lizzy. Is he in the workshop?"

"What do you think?" Lizzy opened her mouth like she was going to say something more. Then she closed it. "I'm going to bed."

Dad was so caught up in our invention that I think he forgot how mad he was at me. The minute he saw me, he started showing me things on the Multishower. We worked together on it until midnight, when I reminded him I was still in school.

The next morning, Dad and I squeezed in 30 minutes on the shower-stall door, while Lizzy cleaned the barn for me. And I still got to duck out 15 minutes early to meet Kaylee before school. We agreed to bike to Bandit's pasture as soon as school was out. Dad—and Madeline— was driving to Mansfield this afternoon. Dad wouldn't be home until suppertime.

School dragged through the day, with the worst hour passing in Ms. Brumby's class. Some of the kids had already written their how-to speeches for the science fair. Ms. Brumby made all of us work on our introductions. Even though I got to partner with Barker, I got so nervous that I couldn't remember the name of my own invention.

At lunch, Sal and Hawk sat with Catman, M, Kaylee, and me to plan my horse birthday party.

"Did you know I talked with Lizzy?" Sal asked. "She's going to make cake and punch. So Hawk and I will just show up with our horses."

They talked about horse games they'd worked up. Sal had even invited Grant and Eager Star.

"Summer said Scarlet Lady would hate the party, so she may not come," Hawk said.

Note to self: Scar isn't all bad.

I still felt weird about having a birthday party. But I had to admit it was starting to sound like fun.

The weather couldn't have been more perfect as Kaylee and I biked to Happy Trails after school. Trees had greened up overnight, sprouting buds like new spring clothes. Jonquils were popping in yards and along the roadside.

We hid our bikes in a ditch and circled to the back pasture, where we found Bandit standing in the same spot as the night before.

Kaylee discovered an empty water bucket tipped over into tall grass inside the fence. We took it to the pond in the main pasture, filled it, and brought it out to Bandit.

The buckskin refused to investigate as long as we were in the pasture, so we climbed out.

Immediately he walked up and took long drinks that nearly emptied the bucket.

"I don't think Leonard will bother with Bandit for a while," I told Kaylee. "So our job is to let your horse know that from now on he can count on gentle handling from people who love him."

"Just tell me what to do," Kaylee said.

"Okay." I grinned at her. "You start." I pulled my paperback copy of *Black Beauty* out of my pocket and handed it to her. "You get the first chapter."

Kaylee didn't even question my tactics. She followed me under the fence and took a seat next to me, a few yards from Bandit. Then she began reading.

As Kaylee read, I watched Bandit out of the corner of my eye. At first he flattened his ears back, daring us to come any closer. After a few pages, his flank stopped twitching, and I saw him flick his tail. By the time Kaylee was done with the first chapter, Bandit's ears were flicking to her voice. He was getting used to us. He was getting a glimpse of the friendlier world we were trying to draw him into.

I read the next chapter, and let Kaylee watch her horse.

When I finished, Kaylee whispered, "He looks more like the old Bandit, Winnie."

"He's learning to trust you, Kaylee." I stood up slowly.

Bandit arched his neck, ready to flee.

"That's enough for one sitting," I said. "Tomorrow we'll get him to join our herd." Mom had taught me the Advance and Retreat method of horse gentling, using a round fenced-in area. It was a technique horse handlers, like the famous Monty Roberts, had picked up by observing the way horses interact in herds. Bandit wouldn't have a real round pen. But the fence and the hedge-apple trees formed a pretty small circle we could work in.

I might have been wrong, but on Wednesday after school, when Kaylee and I got to the out-pasture, it felt like Bandit was waiting for us. He even came up to drink while we stood next to the bucket.

But when Kaylee reached out her hand to pat him, Bandit took off at a gallop. He raced around the pasture, his tail held high.

"Think like a horse, Kaylee," I said, trying to remember how Mom had explained horse gentling to me. "We want Bandit to join up with us and share the safety and happiness of our herd. Bandit wants it too, although he doesn't realize it yet, because all he can see when he looks at us is Leonard. He can't see us. Not yet."

"I'm not sure I get it," Kaylee admitted.

I tried again. "Every herd has a leader. You need to become the leader your horse is looking for. Bandit has to learn to trust again. Then he can discover what it's like to share the joy and safety of a herd."

We moved to the center of the circle as Bandit cantered around us. Eventually he slowed to a walk.

"You have to use your body to talk to him," I explained. "Walk toward him. Hold out your arms and look him in the eye. Scuffle your feet a little until he speeds up again."

Kaylee did exactly what I wanted her to. Bandit took off, galloping in the circle.

"Good! Facing Bandit and looking in his eyes means 'go away.' "

"But I don't want him to go away," she complained.

"No. But you want Bandit to make the decision to join us. Look for his language."

"What am I looking for?" she asked.

"A rotating ear, a droopy neck. He might lick his mouth or lower his head." I remembered seeing those signs with Mom's Mustangs time after time.

"There!" Kaylee whispered. "He's lowering his head, right?"

Bandit did more than that. He slowed down and peeked at Kaylee.

"He's thinking about you," I whispered. "He's looking past that memory of Leonard and wondering what kind of a leader you'd be. Now when he turns to you again, back away from him. Drop your arms, and look down. Moving away is like a reward, and it draws him to you."

It happened again. This time Bandit slowed to a walk and stared at Kaylee. Kaylee saw it and did exactly as I'd told her to do.

Bandit took a few steps toward Kaylee. Then he changed his mind and walked the other way.

"Step toward him again!" I shouted. "Look right at him. Square your body."

This sent the buckskin cantering in a circle again. But it didn't last long. After a couple of laps, Bandit stopped and eyed Kaylee. He licked his lips.

On my cue Kaylee slanted her shoulder away from him and looked away.

Bandit walked straight toward us.

"That's perfect, Kaylee!" I whispered. "You're showing him you want to be friends, but you'll wait on him to decide if he wants to follow you. This is your friendly position, arms and eyes down, turned a little from him. He's thinking of you and how much he'd like to share what we've got going in this herd."

Suddenly Bandit turned away and started to walk off.

"Okay. Back to unfriendly position, Kaylee!" I called. "Arms out at your sides. Look at him and walk toward him."

Kaylee did, and Bandit took off, running in the circle. But after one lap, he slowed to a walk and eyed Kaylee. Again he licked his lips.

"Now!" I whispered. "Back to friendly. Talk to him in a low voice."

Kaylee dropped her arms, looked down, and backed away from Bandit. "Hey, Bandit. You can trust me. Come on, boy."

Bandit stepped toward her. Then his head lowered, and he followed her all the way to the center of our circle.

Kaylee kept up a steady stream of talk.

"Now slowly move toward him," I whispered. "If he doesn't run off, reward him by backing away again."

Kaylee did it exactly right, and Bandit wasn't spooked at all. He followed her, moving closer and closer.

"Hold out your hand and let him smell you," I instructed. "No, the back of your hand."

Just like I'd hoped, Bandit stretched out his neck and sniffed Kaylee's hand.

"Now walk toward me," I called.

Wherever Kaylee walked, Bandit followed.

"This is so amazing," Kaylee whispered. "Winnie, I've never seen anything like it."

I'd seen it quite a few times before, but I felt the same awe Kaylee did. Bandit had joined up. I could already see him getting a piece of the joy that comes from identifying with the herd.

On the ride back Kaylee couldn't stop talking about Leonard and what he might have done to Bandit to make the buckskin so angry at humans. "It's driving me crazy that I haven't heard back from the animal-protection people," she complained. "Do you know when that animal-shelter friend of yours gets back?"

"Ralph? Not until next week."

"I left the address of Happy Trails and a long message on the ASPCA voice mail," she explained. "They have to send somebody out to investigate sooner or later. I just want it to be sooner."

"Me too." A picture flashed into my mind. My brain had snapped a photo of Bandit and Leonard in the barn. Leonard was yanking on the leadrope, as Bandit, tense and terrified, tried to pull away.

"Until the animal-protection people get here, Kaylee, it's up to us. And you and I won't let Leonard near that horse. We won't let anything bad happen to Buckskin Bandit. He's part of our herd now."

Chapter
14

If anything, Thursday's gentling session with Bandit went even better than Wednesday's. By the time I got back from Happy Trails and sat down to a big Lizzy dinner, I was feeling pretty good about everything. Bandit had definitely joined up and would be ready to ride in a day or two. Dad and I had installed the last shower-head on the Magnificent Multishower. And nobody at school had laughed at me when Ms. Brumby made me give my how-to introduction in English class.

Geri was eating dinner with us, so Lizzy dished out four plates of pizza burgers and mozzarella sticks. "Thanks for always seeing that we have enough to make dinner and eat with friends in our home," Lizzy said. Anybody listening in would have thought Lizzy was talking to Dad. But we knew she was talking to God. Lizzy prays as naturally as a Tennessee Walking Horse walks. "Thanks that Kaylee and Winnie are helping that poor horse. Oh, and look out for everybody tomorrow at the science fair. Amen."

"Tomorrow's the big day!" Dad exclaimed as he dished up applesauce. "Winnie, we'll need to set up bright and early. I have it all arranged with the janitor."

"Will you stay for the judging, Dad?" I asked. I still dreaded the speech part of the fair. I was counting on the Multishower speaking for itself.

"Are you kidding? Would I miss the debut of Willis and Willis Inventors?"

"Willis and Willis and Willis, you mean," Geri said, helping herself to another burger.

"What's that, Geri?" Dad asked.

"Didn't Lizzy tell you?" Geri took a gulp of milk. "She's entered in the science fair too."

Dad nearly choked on his grape drink. "Lizzy? You entered the science fair? But I thought it was just for middle schools."

"That's what we thought too," Geri explained. "Only our science teacher said other schools counted sixth grade in their middle schools, and it wasn't fair that we didn't get to participate with the seventh and eighth graders just because Ashland sticks sixth graders with lower grades. And the science fair gives an award for each class. So we get to do it."

"Well, good for you!" Dad exclaimed.

"What can you guys invent on such short notice?" I asked.

"Oh, we've known about it all week," Geri answered. "I'm inventing frog spray. Only it's not working so well."

"Why didn't you tell us you were inventing something, Lizzy?" Dad asked.

"It's not a big deal," Lizzy said, getting up to clear her dishes. "I'm just using something I already had."

"What?" I asked.

"Lizzy's entering the sleeping-bag tent!" Geri announced.

"I love that invention, Lizzy," Dad said. "Good for you." He got up and threw his dishes into the sink. "Now, if you'll excuse us, girls, Winnie and I have a few finishing touches to put on the Magnificent Multishower."

As it turned out, the "few finishing touches"

took us until midnight. Then I had to wash my hair and go over what I'd say to the judges. I could hear Dad whistling from the workshop for another hour. I just hoped I wouldn't let him down.

When I finally crawled into bed, I remembered. Tomorrow was Lizzy's birthday. At the Ashland Public Library sale, I'd managed to pick up six books on lizards. I sneaked them out of the closet and wrapped the books in Sunday's comics.

"Winnie? What time is it?" Lizzy sounded like she was underwater.

"Really late," I whispered. "Or really early, depending on how you look at it. Happy birthday, Lizzy."

Lizzy rolled over and leaned on one elbow. "Sweet! We're the same age."

"Want your presents?" I asked, feeling like we were two instead of 12.

Lizzy grinned. She reminded me of our mom so much it hurt. "Presents? As in plural? I like the sound of that! Bring 'em on."

I handed the books to her one by one, and she squealed like a little kid as she ripped off the paper.

"I can't believe you found *Lizards I Have*

Known!" she screamed. "I *love* that book!" She stretched out her arms, and I came closer so she could hug me. "Thanks, Winnie."

"Lizzy, I'm sorry . . . about birthdays, I mean."

"We're past that. Right? Sal and Hawk are putting together quite a party for you, you know. And I'm going over to Geri's tomorrow night to celebrate my birthday—I mean, tonight."

"That's great, Lizzy." I was glad she'd have something special to do on her birthday. Maybe next year I'd have a huge birthday party for my sister.

We lay in bed for a while, talking and remembering birthdays when we were little kids. Finally, we both dropped off to sleep.

"Rise and shine, young inventors!" Dad shouted.

I felt as if I'd just gotten to sleep. It wasn't even light outside.

"Winnie, we have to get to school early and set up the Magnificent Multishower. After today, America will be a cleaner place to live!"

I rolled over to tell Lizzy happy birthday again, but she was already up.

"Lizzy loved her gecko home," Dad said. "Made it myself, according to all the specifications. Built the lighting myself too. Madeline gave Lizzy a gift certificate to Pat's Pets for one gecko."

"Great gift, Dad," I said, wondering why Dad couldn't have gotten Lizzy the gecko gift certificate himself. We're not that poor.

"We should have made a birthday cake," he said.

"I know."

"Well, hurry up! And don't forget to wear something nice."

I was just glad Dad didn't expect me to wear a one-piece work suit like he wears when he's inventing. I groped around for a clean pair of jeans and a shirt that wasn't too wrinkled.

Before leaving to meet Geri at school, Lizzy had made bacon and scrambled eggs with olives and cheese. But I barely had time to take a bite before Dad was honking the horn.

Dad and I were the first people in the gym except for Mr. Jay, our school janitor. We rolled the shower stall close to the exit, then ran the hose outside to the spigot. All I'd have to do was turn on the faucet, and we'd be in business. We tried it out, and it worked just like it had at home.

Other parents and kids filed in and set up their booths all around the gym. I practiced my speech in my head, while Dad polished the showerheads.

"Dad, I hope I don't mess up."

Dad stopped polishing and frowned over at me. "What do you mean, Winnie?"

"I'm not the greatest talker in the world, Dad, in case you haven't noticed. No matter how great the invention is, if I can't tell the judges about it, they won't choose me."

"Nonsense. You'll do just fine." Dad went back to the showerhead. Then he reached over and squeezed my shoulder. "I'll . . . I'll be praying for you, Winnie."

I felt like I'd swallowed something too big for my throat. Dad had never said anything like that to me. When we'd lived in Wyoming, Mom was the one who made all four of us go to church every Sunday. But when Mom died, Dad stopped going to church. Lizzy still went with friends, but I'd stayed home with Dad.

Even when we moved to Ashland, for a long time Lizzy was the only one who went to church. Then I started going. And then Dad. He'd been going with us since last fall, but he still didn't talk about God much.

"Thanks, Dad." It's all I was able to squeeze past whatever was stuck in my throat.

Dad seemed to be looking at my feet. He reminded me of Kaylee, right before Bandit joined up with her. I reached over and gave my dad a short, awkward hug.

"Think I'll check out the competition," he said. And he strolled off.

I read over my notes, stopping to wave at the Barkers. M's parents, both dressed totally in black like M, came by to wish me luck. So did Mr. and Mrs. Coolidge. Mrs. Coolidge was carrying Churchill, Catman's biggest cat, a gray shorthair, with a face as flat as a silver dollar. Mr. Coolidge had the squirmy Bumby, a small black cat with huge white paws and six toes in front, seven in back. I figured the cats would be demonstrating Catman's cat bunks.

"Winnie!"

I looked up to see Lizzy and Geri trekking through the crowd. Lizzy had her sleeping bag slung over her shoulder. "You guys better get set up!" I called.

Lizzy looked so cute. She'd french-braided her hair and was wearing khakis with a red, flowered shirt I hadn't seen before. Geri, of course, was dressed in frog green.

"Do you think this smells like frog?" Geri asked, shoving a bottle of slime-green liquid under my nose.

I tried not to gag. It smelled like pond scum. "Sure reminds me of frogs, Geri."

"Sweet!" Geri exclaimed.

Lizzy had to run and say hi to some kids in her class. Geri hung back with me. "Winnie, where's your dad? I've been planning a surprise party for Lizzy after the science fair."

"That's great, Geri!" And I meant it.

"But both of my parents pulled the night shift. So I can't have it at our house. Can I have it at yours, do you think?"

Dad was strolling back to the booth. I waved to him to hurry up. "I'll bet it's okay. Let's ask Dad."

Dad was so distracted he'd have agreed to having a horse show in his workshop. "It won't be any work for you guys," Geri promised. "My mom made a cake. And Nathan is bringing pop. And . . ." Geri ran through all the refreshments and games and a list of kids coming. Then she raced off to find Lizzy. My sister was really lucky to have so many friends.

Dad walked off to ask Mr. Jay about water pressure. I was going over my speech when Hawk walked in with Peter Lory, her chattering lory. Every kid seemed to turn and look at her. And the guys weren't looking at Peter, either.

We waved and hollered hi, but her booth was at the other end of the gym.

Kaylee came over to my booth. "All set, Winnie?"

"I guess. How about you?"

She shrugged. "I've seen four other kids with my exact same exhibit. Guess what! I got up early this morning and biked out to see Bandit. He's doing great, Winnie. Can we do another training session later? I can't get away until eight. Would that work?"

"Sure. Come to my house first. We'll go together." I knew, with all the friends Lizzy would be having over, they'd never miss me.

The PA system screeched. "Will the parents

please move to the south end of the gym? We ask that you remain behind the yellow line while our students have their exhibits judged."

I got in position and saw that directly across from me was M's booth. We exchanged wordless hellos. All he had on his table was a shiny black ball bigger than a softball.

I raised my eyebrows at him. He twitched his nose. Then he picked up the ball and turned it upside down. I dashed across the aisle for a better look. The ball looked like Magic 8 fortune balls I'd seen when I was a kid back in Wyoming. Only instead of dumb "predictions," like "It is decidedly so," M's ball carried on a conversation: "What's your favorite kind of art?" "Which person had the biggest influence on your life?" "What's the most important thing in your life?" "How important is God in your life?" "If you died tonight, where would go?" "How would you change the world?"

"M!" I exclaimed. "This is awesome! How did you make the ball?"

"Pottery wheel," he answered.

"What's the green stuff the questions are floating in?" I asked.

"Jell-O."

I grinned approval at M and ran back to my booth.

Aisles grew quiet as the judges moved up and down. I could hear kids explaining their inventions to the team of three judges. Summer almost sang her speech, running her finger-combs through her hair. Catman was too far away for me to hear him, but I spotted Churchill chasing Bumby under the tables.

When the judges came to M, the tall, sharp-nosed, redheaded woman judge eyed him up and down. The second judge, a big man with kind eyes, shook M's ball and laughed hard. The third judge, with fair skin and hair that may have been blond once but looked white now, was quiet. In my mind, the judges became American Saddle Horse Woman, Clydesdale Man, and Palomino.

The closer they got to me, the more I wanted to bolt from the gym. One more booth, and they'd be right in front of me.

American Saddle Horse Woman walked up first. "And you must be—" she checked her clip-board, then flipped a page—"Winifred Willis."

"Winnie?" I said, like I was asking her.

The other two judges flanked in behind her,

but Saddle Horse was definitely in charge. "Please tell us about this interesting-looking invention," she said, moving closer to inspect the shower.

"It's a . . . a Multiple Shower," I said, trying to remember our official name for the thing.

Clydesdale Man cleared his throat. "Excuse me?"

I cleared my throat too. But of course it didn't do me any good. "Multiple Shower?"

"Ah," said Palomino. "What does it do?"

"It . . ." Every thought flew out of my head. What *did* it do? I tried to picture my note card, my introduction. But my stupid brain camera hadn't bothered to take a picture of that. "Like, g-gets you really clean?" I stammered.

"And how did you come up with this idea?" Saddle Horse asked.

I'd planned to say something about the guy who cried "Eureka!" But I couldn't remember the whole story. "That guy in the bathtub," I said. "I mean, when the water splashed and he ran down the street screaming."

They stared at me as if I had multiple heads.

I shot up a prayer that God would calm down my brain. Then I tried again, telling them about the junkyard and Dad being an inventor and cutting holes in the stall and everything.

They listened. Saddle Horse Woman jotted notes on her clipboard. Then they thanked me and walked on.

"Wait!" I shouted. "I forgot to turn it on!"

Saddle Horse fake-smiled over her shoulder. "That's all right, dear."

And I knew. In those few horrible seconds I'd wrecked the entire future of Willis and Willis Inventors.

$\mathcal{D}$ad waved at me over the heads of other parents who were straining to hear the judges. I tried to smile as I waved back. He didn't know it was all over, but I did.

Minutes later another screech shot from the PA system. The crowd let out one big groan. Then the voice of our principal, Mr. Russell, boomed through the gym. "Ladies and gentlemen! Places, please. We are ready to announce the winners of the Ashland Middle School Science Fair!"

If you hadn't met Mr. Russell, who's thin, wiry, and about Lizzy's height, you would have thought, by his voice, that you were listening to another Clydesdale Man. I think it's from all those years of hollering, "Don't run in the halls!"

Note to self: Try hollering in the halls. Maybe it will help your voice.

"We've had an excellent show today!" Mr. Russell boomed.

Parents applauded.

"And now I'll turn over the mike to Ms. Brandywine, one of our judges. She will announce one winner from each grade who will represent AMS in the state competition tomorrow in Columbus."

I glanced at Dad, and he held up crossed fingers.

Ms. Brandywine turned out to be American Saddle Horse Woman. "Thank you, Principal Russell. We shall begin with the eighth-grade division. The winning invention is the Conversation Ball. The inventor is . . . M? I'm sorry. That's all I have on my card. Could someone—?"

But applause thundered around the gym, drowning out Saddle Horse Woman. M's parents were screaming the loudest.

Finally, with Principal Russell's help, we quieted down enough for them to continue. "And now we have a winner for the seventh-grade division."

My stomach hurt. It felt like I imagined colic must feel to a horse.

"The winner is . . . Summer Spidell, for her finger-combs and brushes."

I should have known.

Dad's face looked like melting ice cream, his features running down to his chin. When we saw each other, his face snapped back like elastic. But it was too late. I'd already seen how disappointed he was.

He waved, and I waved back, both of us faking a smile and a shrug.

He would have been so proud to have a winner for a daughter. Willis and Willis Inventors. It had been nice while it lasted.

"And finally," Saddle Horse was saying, "in the sixth-grade division, the winner is . . . Elizabeth Willis, for the sleeping-bag tent."

"Lizzy! Lizzy! Lizzy!" The chant broke out all over the gym.

Stunned, I turned to see Dad pushing through the crowd that thronged toward my sister's booth. He was cheering louder than everybody put together. "That's my daughter! That's my Lizzy!"

Catman and Barker crowded around and congratulated her.

Hawk joined them and shook Lizzy's hand.

It seemed the whole world was excited for Lizzy. I tried to be too. I was. Really. Only it hadn't meant that much to Lizzy.

And it had meant a lot to me.

By the time I managed to push my way through the crowd around Lizzy, she and Dad were smiling for the cameras, which flashed like nonstop lightning.

"My dad is the real inventor," Lizzy said to a woman from the *Ashland Times Gazette*.

"Congratulations, Lizzy!" I yelled up.

Lizzy waved and gave me a go-figure shrug.

"Plus," Geri shouted to the reporter, "this is Lizzy's birthday! She won on her birthday!"

Dad was shaking Principal Russell's hand.

The principal, grinning, shouted, "I'd love to come, Willis! Thanks!"

I hoped Dad hadn't just invited my principal to our house. Our whole house would probably fit in Principal Russell's basement. And he'd have to refinish it.

Hawk slid through a crowd of teachers to get back to me. "I am really looking forward to our horse birthday party tomorrow, Winnie."

It was a nice thing to say. I felt like Hawk

knew what was going on inside me as I watched Lizzy and Dad together. Hawk had been trying to get her dad's attention ever since the divorce. And she hadn't had much luck either.

Suddenly all I wanted to do was go for a long ride on Nickers. I needed to forget about inventions, and Willis and Willis, and everything except the pounding of my horse's hooves.

We were allowed to go home for the day after the science fair. But Dad kept talking and talking, until almost the whole gym had emptied. As soon as the last teacher quit congratulating Dad, I moved up. "Dad, I'll just walk home. I want to ride Nickers."

Dad frowned. "Not today, Winnie. Too much to do." He leaned down and whispered, "We're having a surprise party for Lizzy."

"I know," I answered. "I'll be back later."

Dad shook his head. "You'll need the rest of the afternoon to get the house in shape, honey. I've invited all of Lizzy's teachers. And your principal. And . . . I can't remember who else. We'll need more food. What can you make for snacks?"

"Me?"

"I'll help all I can, honey. But I have to help

Lizzy work out a couple of kinks in her invention before tomorrow."

I wanted to shout that it wasn't fair. But he was already running over to Lizzy's sleeping-bag tent.

Note to self: The distance from Willis the Inventor to Willis the Slave is about 20 seconds.

I walked home and still got there two hours before Dad and Lizzy drove up. Instead of galloping across the pasture, I'd spent my time vacuuming, dusting, scrubbing the toilet, and mopping the kitchen floor. The house still looked like a herd of Mustangs lived in it.

Lizzy and Dad strolled through the front door, laughing. Neither of them said a word about all the work I'd done in the house. They headed for Dad's workshop. The workshop door shut, and I went back to Lizzy's chores.

Note to self: Just call me Winnie-ella.

Geri was the first to show up for the party, followed by her mom, who was carrying a giant birthday cake. They brought sandwiches too, which was a good thing, because my applesauce muffins looked more like horse-apple muffins.

Madeline came early too. She'd left Mason, her better half, at home with a babysitter. She carried in two grocery bags of pop and potato chips.

By six o'clock our house was so full of people that we had to leave the doors open. Hawk came over and helped me pass out food, pick up dishes, and clean up spills. Conversations buzzed around me, most of them about my sister. Dad didn't leave Lizzy's side the whole time.

At exactly eight Kaylee fought her way inside. "Winnie, are you ready?"

I'd almost forgotten about Bandit's lesson. "We better make a quick getaway," I whispered, setting down my tray of muffins.

I'd almost made it to the door when Dad shouted across the room, "Winnie! Better bring out a pitcher of water!"

"Wait here," I whispered to Kaylee.

But three water pitchers and a bag of Oreos later, I wasn't any closer to freedom. I'd have to level with Dad.

He was talking with a broad, black-haired woman, who reminded me of a Morgan horse. I had to tap on Dad's arm to make him see me. "Dad, Kaylee's here. We're going to Happy Trails to check on Bandit."

"Not tonight, honey." He turned back to Morgan Woman.

"Dad? We won't be long. Just leave everything. I'll clean up when I get back."

Dad leaned down and gave me eye contact this time. "Winnie, Lizzy needs you tonight."

There were a hundred answers that came to my mind. All of them would have gotten me in trouble.

I stormed back to Kaylee, bumping as many guests as I could on the way.

"I can't go. I'm sorry, Kaylee." I glared back at Dad, but he was laughing with Lizzy and Morgan Woman.

"Don't worry about it," Kaylee said. "I'll just run out there and say good night to Bandit."

"Well, be careful. And tomorrow, right after the horse birthday party, we can give Bandit a long lesson."

I watched Kaylee go and wished more than anything that I could escape with her. Instead,

I grabbed a tray of ugly muffins and hit the living room.

Principal Russell reached for a muffin as I walked by. He frowned at it, then put it back. "You must be pretty happy for your little sister. Quite an honor to go to State. Are you excited about going to Columbus tomorrow?"

"I'm sure Lizzy will do great," I said. And I was sure. Lizzy would probably come home with first prize. "I'm not going to Columbus, though."

"What?" Dad turned around, breaking off his conversation with Lizzy's teacher and Madeline. "Of course you're going, Winnie! Lizzy needs our support."

"Dad, did you forget what tomorrow is?" I hated arguing in front of the principal. "Hawk and Sal and everybody are coming over in the morning with their horses. For a party. Remember?"

"That's right," Dad said. "I forgot. We'll just have to make it for another day, honey. Okay? I can't have a party here if I'm not home to supervise. We'll do it right—maybe next Saturday?"

I could feel my blood ready to overflow in hot, red lava. "Dad, it's all planned."

Hawk walked up without a sound.

"You can plan it for another day," Dad insisted. "Right, Hawk?"

"But that's not fair!" I said it loud enough that heads turned. "You don't even need me in Columbus."

"That may be true, Winnie," Dad answered.

It wasn't the answer I wanted. I wanted him to protest, to say, "Are you kidding, Winnie? Lizzy and I both need you!"

But Dad *didn't* say that. He pretended to smile, even though he had to know he wasn't fooling any of the people trying not to witness our family. "This discussion is over. There will be no party here while I am out of town."

"But—"

"Winnie, will you please go make more coffee?" Dad said it through his teeth. Translated, it meant, *Winnie, don't you dare pull a temper tantrum on me in front of all these people.*

"Come on, Winnie." Hawk took my arm and led me away. "I'll call everybody. We can do the party next week. Or the week after that?"

But I wasn't listening. Blood was rushing through my ears. I had a lot more to say to my dad. And I didn't care who heard me.

"Dad? Could you come here a minute?" Lizzy called from the workshop.

Dad sprung up from the couch. "Coming, Lizzy!"

And just like that, he was gone.

Note to self: "Unfair" equals one sister who gets the good hair, the good height, the winning invention, the birthday party . . . and our dad.

Lizzy and Dad went to bed as soon as the guests left. I was finishing washing dishes when the phone rang.

Kaylee started talking the second I said hello. "I'm sorry to bother you so late, Winnie. But I can't stand it. I don't know what to do!"

"Kaylee, what's the matter?"

"It's Bandit! Oh, Winnie, they're going to get rid of him!"

 $\mathcal{K}$ aylee was so upset that it took a few
minutes before I could understand her over the
phone. She'd taken the back route to Happy
Trails, just like we'd done all week. Then she'd
hung out with Bandit awhile. She was ready to
leave when she heard voices. So she hid behind
the bank of hedge-apple trees. That's when
she'd heard Leonard talking to another man
about getting rid of the buckskin.

Over the phone, Kaylee let out a sigh that
came through my receiver like a galloping wind.
"Oh, Winnie, you should have heard them. The
other man, Reggie, told Leonard the animal-
protection investigator would be coming out
tomorrow afternoon. And Leonard said, 'Then
we better get rid of that buckskin tomorrow

morning!' Winnie, what does he mean 'get rid of'? What are they going to do to Bandit?"

The kitchen was still, silent, except for the clock ticking. I wanted to run to the pasture right then and rescue Bandit. But I couldn't do anything, not tonight. "They're not going to do anything, Kaylee. I'll be at your house at dawn. We won't let them do anything to Buckskin Bandit."

Dad and Lizzy would have to go to Columbus without me. They probably wouldn't even notice the difference.

I might have dozed off for a couple of hours. But I got up while it was still pitch-black outside. Nickers whinnied to me as I hurried to the barn under a fading moon. Stars spread across the black sky in odd-shaped groups, like herds banding together.

The minute I stepped into the barn, I remembered it was my birthday. I was 13.

Note to self (since nobody else will): Happy Birthday to me. Right.

Buddy and Nickers crowded into the stall and

waited for their morning oats. Annie stamped her hoof until I fed her. After a minute, Towaco joined us in the barn, and I quickly brushed the three horses, leaving the stalls for later. I wanted to be gone before Lizzy and Dad found out I was missing.

I'd left them a note on the kitchen table, where Lizzy always leaves us notes:

Good luck, Lizzy. I'm sure you'll come home with a trophy. Sorry I can't come with you. I have urgent horse business here. Dad, please don't be mad. Kaylee really needs me this morning, and you guys really don't. I'll be fine here. —Love, Winnie

I slipped on Nickers' hackamore and led her away from the house before swinging onto her back. Light began breaking through the sky, swallowing up the star herds. I leaned on Nickers' neck as she walked through the pasture toward Kaylee's side of town. I didn't have to think when I rode Nickers. We felt each other. We'd joined up a long time ago, and we'd stayed that way.

God, I prayed, feeling guilty that I hadn't talked to God much lately, *I know you and I joined up too. But right now I don't know where I belong or who I belong to.*

My mind flashed me a picture of Lizzy standing with Dad as the cameras flashed around her in the school gym. Lizzy's smile took in her whole face. She was so happy.

So why did I feel so sad? Pat's magnetic verse popped into my head, along with the smiling picture of Lizzy: *"When others are happy, be happy with them."*

How do I do that, God? I prayed. *When I see Lizzy and Dad smiling together, all I can do is wish I could be the one standing next to Dad. How can I be happy with them?*

Kaylee was waiting by the road when Nickers and I trotted up.

"Winnie, thanks for coming! I couldn't sleep all night. What's the plan?"

"We'll ride to Happy Trails, and we won't let them take Buckskin Bandit," I promised. That was about as far as I'd gotten with the plan.

But Kaylee grinned, as if I'd just offered the best solution in the world. Then she hopped up behind me, and we cantered most of the way to Happy Trails.

In no time we were crossing the field to Bandit's pasture. Bandit nickered, and Nickers answered.

"Shh-h-h," I told Nickers. "The last thing we want to do is wake Leonard."

We got off and walked to the fence. Bandit didn't even wait for us to whistle. He trotted up, his tail high and nostrils wide.

Kaylee dug out a carrot from her pocket, and Bandit chomped it, while I let Nickers graze. "Now what?" Kaylee asked.

I didn't have an answer. Now that we were here, I wasn't sure what to do. If Leonard came for Bandit, how could Kaylee and I stop him?

Kaylee was looking to me for our next move. "Winnie? How exactly are we going to keep them from taking Bandit away?"

"We're . . . we're going to beat them to it!" I said. The idea had burst into my head, just like that.

I ran to the gate. Kaylee and I hadn't used it, but Bandit would need to. "We're going to get Bandit away from Happy Trails," I said, wishing I'd thought to bring a long leadrope.

"Steal him?" Kaylee asked.

"No! Rescue him," I answered. "We'll keep him at my barn until the animal inspector shows up. We can tell Ralph too."

I tried the latch, but it wouldn't budge. Then I saw the padlock. "It's locked!" I cried, glancing frantically around the tiny fence. There was no other way out.

Bandit was trapped.

"Kaylee! We'll have to ride back and get hoof cutters. Maybe a wire cutter too." I called Nickers and jumped on her bareback. "Stand on that log, and I'll ride by for you."

Kaylee didn't move. "I'm not leaving Bandit," she said quietly.

"Kaylee! I can't leave you here!"

She shook her head. "I'll wait with Bandit, Winnie. Lazy Lenny won't show up this early. Go!"

I didn't like leaving her. But she was right. I'd be back in plenty of time. "Okay. But if anybody comes, hide. Don't be a hero."

She nodded.

"And I'll bring a bridle. Do you think you could ride Bandit to my barn?"

"Bareback?" she asked, glancing at the buckskin, who stuck his head over the fence to be scratched. "I've never ridden without a saddle, except behind you. I've never even ridden anywhere except this trail."

"I'll bring a saddle," I said. "Back in a flash."

Nickers pivoted, rearing front legs a foot off the ground. Then she took off in a dead gallop. We flew back through the fields, across the pasture, all the way home. The truck was gone, just as I'd thought. Dad and Lizzy were probably halfway to Columbus by now.

In the barn I gathered tools into an old saddlebag. I tossed a leadrope, a hackamore, and a snaffle bridle into another bag. Kaylee wouldn't feel safe unless she rode with a saddle, so I pulled out my lightest saddle, the one Pat had given me when I'd started as Winnie the Horse Gentler.

By the time I finished gathering everything, I couldn't carry it. I'd taken too long. I had to get back to Kaylee and Bandit.

"Winnie? What are you doing here?"

I dropped the saddle and turned to see none other than Madeline Edison.

$\mathcal{M}$adeline towered over me in the dim light of the barn. "Winnie Willis, what are you doing here? You should be in Columbus!"

"I-I . . . Columbus," I stammered.

"Does your father know where you are?" she asked.

"Well, kind of."

She reached into her purse and pulled out her cell phone. "Jack is probably worried about you."

"Wait, Madeline!" I pleaded.

She kept the phone poised but didn't dial. "What's going on, Winnie? Where are you going with all that stuff?"

"This stuff?"

Madeline stepped closer, and I saw Mason behind her.

"Hey, Mason!" I called, hoping he could

distract his mother until I could think of a good explanation for her.

Mason was staring up at the barn ceiling so intently, I could imagine him boring holes through the roof.

"Winnie, I'm waiting for an answer." Her finger moved toward the phone buttons.

"I know," I said. "Just give me a minute to say hey to Mason. Okay?" I knelt down, Mason-height, and tried to think. "Did you come to see Buddy?" I asked him.

He didn't move. His body looked as stiff as a three-gaited show horse. Mason was in one of his zones. He'd escaped to a place where nobody could reach him.

Madeline put her hand on her son's head. "He was fine yesterday, until nighttime. I don't think he shut his eyes the whole night. I thought if I brought him over here, maybe Buddy could snap him out of it again."

I stared into Mason's eyes. They were deep pools, with nobody there. "Buddy's been missing you, Mason. Want to go see her?" I put my hand on Mason's shoulder.

He jerked away. Then he let out a scream that didn't sound human. It froze my spine. He kept it up so long I thought he'd faint from not breathing.

"I'm sorry," I said when the scream finally died out. I put my hands in my pockets to keep them from shaking.

"It's not your fault," Madeline said. "He'll be all right. We'll just let him have time. Isn't that right, Mason?"

Mason didn't answer.

She turned to me. "Now, Winnie, I think you better tell me what exactly is going on."

Time was running out. Kaylee was back at Happy Trails, guarding Bandit from Leonard and who knew what else. Madeline had her phone in dialing position again. I had no choice. I had to tell her.

As quickly as I could, I told Madeline everything. About Kaylee. About Bandit. About Leonard.

"We couldn't just let Leonard get rid of Bandit!" I pleaded. "He hurt that buckskin, Madeline. And Bandit's just starting to get over it, to trust people again."

Please, God! Please make her understand!

"And Kaylee's there at Happy Trails right now?" Madeline asked.

I nodded. I stared at the phone, still clutched in her fist. "Are you going to call Dad?"

Madeline looked back at Mason, who hadn't budged during my whole account. Then she shook her head slowly. "I'm not saying that I won't tell him later, Winnie. And actually, you should be the one to do that. But right now I think you better get back to that horse."

"You do?" I couldn't believe it. She didn't even like horses.

Madeline nodded. "Abuse is a terrible, terrible thing." Her eyes got watery. It was the closest I'd ever seen her to tears. "Well, don't just stand there! Go! Hurry!"

I threw the saddlebag over my shoulder and grabbed the bag of tools. Then I tried to pick up the saddle.

Madeline snatched it out of my hands. "Come on! I'll drive."

"You?"

She grinned. "Consider it a happy-birthday gift."

She'd remembered.

She scooped Mason onto her shoulders and jogged all the way to her van.

We were barely off our street when Mason

fell asleep in his car seat. He's seven, but he's so small that his car seat is toddler-sized.

I watched Madeline as she leaned over the steering wheel and drove faster than Dad would have. I couldn't figure her out. "Why are you being so nice, Madeline?" Then I realized how it sounded. "I mean, not that you're not always nice. It's just . . . why are you helping me?"

She was quiet for so long that I was afraid she was mad at me for saying she wasn't nice all the time. Then she whispered, "Winnie, I think you're old enough to hear what I have to say. I know that you love Mason and would never say anything that would upset him."

She waited for me to nod. I did.

"Have you ever wondered about Mason?" she began. "Why he is the way he is?"

I'd thought about it a lot. I'd even asked Dad. All he'd ever tell me was that something had happened to Mason, something that left him with nerve damage in his brain. "Yes."

Madeline gripped the steering wheel so hard her long fingers went white. "You know I was married before. I married young and unwisely. Then we had a baby. Mason was the cutest baby in the world." She smiled, as if she had a photographic memory too, and was seeing Mason as a little baby right now.

"I'll bet he was a cute baby," I agreed.

She smiled at me. It was funny. She hardly looked like Madeline. Her nose didn't seem so long, and there was nothing odd-looking about her.

"Well, as cute he was," she continued, "our little Mason was a handful. He fussed and cried a lot, but not that much more than other babies. I don't suppose either Miles or I knew much about raising an infant."

Madeline's back stiffened, and she bit her lip and squinted at the road ahead. "Mason's father had a very short fuse. One night, after I'd been up with the baby for hours until he dropped off to sleep, I went back to bed. In the middle of the night I awoke to a thump."

She stopped, and I was afraid she wouldn't finish. I wanted to know. I had to know.

"I ran into the nursery. And there was Mason, lying on the floor next to the wall. He wasn't moving."

My chest burned. I could see Mason as a baby, lying there, and Madeline running to him. I could see it as clearly as if I'd been there.

"Mason's father had thrown his son against the wall to make him stop crying."

I turned around to see Mason. He was asleep, his head leaning back. I could see the dimple on his cheek, and he looked like an angel. How could anybody do that?

"Madeline, I'm sorry." I couldn't say anything else.

"Me too," she said. "It was the last time either of us saw or spoke to his father. For the first year after the divorce, I blamed myself for not seeing it coming. I should have known Miles had violence in him. But I didn't, Winnie. Or maybe I did, but I didn't want to admit it."

"It wasn't your fault," I said, wishing somebody else were in the car with us. Somebody who'd know what to say, like Dad or Lizzy.

"After I was finished blaming myself, I suppose I blamed God, although I wouldn't have said that. I'd look at other boys Mason's age, and I'd get angry all over again. Why should they live normal, happy lives while Mason disappeared into himself almost every day? It wasn't fair."

It wasn't fair. How many times had I said or

thought those exact words in the last couple of weeks?

She was crying softly now and driving so slowly that three cars zoomed past us. "Your dad asks me every week if I'll go to church with him. And every week I turn him down. I guess I haven't finished blaming God yet, have I?"

I knew how she was feeling. I'd blamed myself for Mom's accident. And then I'd blamed God. "Madeline, you didn't hurt Mason. And neither did God. Mason's dad did it." My voice was so raspy that I didn't know if she could understand me.

I glanced back at Mason again. "Look at him, Madeline."

She looked in her rearview mirror and almost ran off the side of the road. But the sight of Mason made her stop crying. Her eyes softened. There was joy written all over her face—in the crinkles under her eyes, in the way her mouth grew soft.

I prayed that I could find the right words. "Madeline, even with all his problems, Mason Edison is the most totally joyful person I've ever met. He makes everyone around him smile. He gets excited about colts. And have you ever seen anybody get so much happiness out of an Appaloosa spot or a smudge on the ceiling?"

She laughed softly, then stopped. "I know you're right, Winnie. But when I see other children playing together . . . I just can't get past that moment when everything changed, when I found Mason on the floor and knew what his father had done to him. That's what I keep seeing, even now."

Madeline didn't have a photographic memory, but she didn't need one. That picture of Mason was burned into her mind as deeply as the picture of Mom's accident was carved into mine. As deeply as the memory of Leonard's cruelty had been stamped into Bandit's brain.

"We're all leaf-blocked." I wasn't sure if I'd said it out loud or not.

Madeline frowned over at me. "What?"

"It's what Catman and M taught me, what they did on our trail ride. They held up a leaf and blocked out the sun." I turned in my seat belt so I could see her better. "Did you know that you can block out a whole sun or moon if you hold a tiny leaf in front of your face?"

Madeline nodded slowly.

"That's what I do—hold the wrong things in front of my face. I'm leaf-blocked, Madeline. I can't see past the leaf." Thoughts were coming fast. I could hardly piece them together for myself. How could I ever make her understand?

"Go on, Winnie," Madeline said. "What are you holding in front of your face?"

"Mom's accident." But I knew there was more. *God, help me get this,* I prayed. "And maybe Lizzy. Lizzy and Dad."

"You mean because Lizzy won at the science fair and you didn't?"

"That, and other stuff. Lizzy's pretty easy to envy."

We both laughed a little. It helped. Maybe I'd been leaf-blocked about Madeline too.

I made myself go on. "When Lizzy won, Dad seemed to forget about me, except when it came to assigning me Lizzy's chores. It felt so unfair."

"But didn't she do your chores when Jack was working on your invention?"

Madeline was right. Totally right. And I hadn't noticed it at all, not even once. Lizzy had cleaned stalls for me while I went off to ride with Kaylee. She'd done her chores and mine for a week. And I'd never once thought of that as unfair. "Guess that's what I mean about not seeing things when you're leaf-blocked."

Madeline glanced at Mason again. "Leaf-blocked. Hmmm. No one else has a more loving son than I do. He's full of surprises, most of them great ones. The little I know about joy, I've learned from Mason."

Her fingers drummed the dashboard. "Leaf-blocked," she repeated. Suddenly she smacked the steering wheel. The car swerved, then straightened out. "Winnie, you may be right about that leaf! I think I'm starting to see the sun."

"I want Buddy," Mason mumbled. He yawned and stretched out his little arms. When he smiled at us, his dimple shone like the sun, filling Madeline's van.

We were almost to Happy Trails. "Madeline, you better stop here," I said.

She pulled the van over to the side of the road, letting one wheel slide into the ditch.

"Thanks for driving me, Madeline," I said, lugging the saddle out of the van and dumping it on the ground. "You don't have to wait or anything. I can come back for the saddle."

"Oh, we're not going to wait, are we, Mason? We're coming with you." She hopped out and started unbuckling Mason's seat belt.

"You shouldn't come, Madeline. We might get in really big trouble. I'm going to have to break the padlock to get Bandit away from here."

"Then it seems to me you're going to need all the help you can get. Now toss me that saddle."

Nobody who saw Madeline Edison for the first time would ever guess how strong she is. With Mason tucked under one arm like a football, she hoisted the saddle under her other arm and took off at a trot toward the back pasture.

I grabbed both bags and ran after her. "That way!" I shouted.

Kaylee and Bandit were waiting at the far end of the pasture. Bandit trailed behind her, as if Kaylee were the herd's dominant mare.

"Looks like a friendly horse," Madeline commented as we got closer.

"You should have seen him a week ago," I said. I thought about how much Bandit had changed. His leaf had come down, and the world looked brighter to him. He was a happy horse again. We couldn't let Leonard ruin that.

Kaylee waved, then dropped her arm and frowned when she saw Madeline.

"She's okay!" I called out. "Madeline's helping!"

"Mason helping too!" he cried.

I reached over and ruffled his hair. "Mason is helping big-time," I agreed.

Madeline set him down and walked up to the pasture fence. "The horse is so skinny. Poor thing."

Kaylee pointed out the scars on Bandit's rump and chest. "Spur marks here. And these have to be whip marks."

Madeline's face got bright red, and her eyes bugged out. "If I get my hands on this . . . this Leonard, he's going to wish he'd never seen a horse!"

I dug out the tools and started to work on the padlock. I tried banging it with the heavy hoof cutters. Then I tried to pry open the lock. Using the wire cutters, I tried cutting the thing off. Nothing worked.

"Hurry, Winnie!" Kaylee shouted.

"I'm trying!"

Suddenly Madeline sprang from the fence and kind of pranced a few feet in the direction of the stable. "Somebody's coming!" she whispered. "Somebody big!"

*L*eonard!" Kaylee and I said at the same time.

"*The* Leonard?" Madeline asked. "The one who hurt Bandit?"

"Bandit's afraid of him!" Kaylee cried. "He says he's going to get rid of my horse!"

Madeline took a big breath. "Oh, he does, does he? You just leave Leonard to me!"

"Be careful!" I shouted.

But Madeline was already storming toward Leonard. Without slowing down, she whipped out her cell phone and dialed. I couldn't tell who she called or what she said. But the conversation took about two seconds. Without losing stride, she shoved the phone back into her purse and closed the gap between Leonard and her.

Mason tried to stomp after his mom, but I

grabbed him. "I need you here, Mason," I said.
"Go help Kaylee with Buckskin Bandit." I guided
him under the fence and into the pasture.
Bandit was a lot safer than Leonard.

I ran to where I could watch Madeline in
action. She charged right up to giant Leonard,
who must have outweighed her 10 times over.
He was carrying a crop, a small whip.

"You there!" she shouted. "Halt!"

Leonard, his beady little eyes doubling in size,
halted.

"How dare you, Leonard!" When Madeline
said it, it sounded like a curse. "How dare you
lay a finger on that lovely horse! How would
you like it if I took the whip and spurs to you?
starved you?" She poked his giant belly as she
delivered this threat.

"Go, Madeline!" I yelled, cheering her on.

"Who are you, lady?" Leonard tried to walk
past her.

Quick as a Quarter Horse, Madeline snatched
the crop out of Leonard's hand. "You get rid of
that nasty whip!"

Leonard tried to grab his crop back. "Lady, I
need to get that crazy animal loaded in my truck
down there. I'm telling you, get out of my way!"

"Over my dead body or yours!" Madeline shouted. "And I'm betting on yours!"

In the distance, I heard a siren.

A big truck at the end of the drive started backing out to the road.

"Reggie!" Leonard screamed. "Get back here!"

But the truck took off in the opposite direction as the siren grew louder and louder.

Mason covered his ears. Bandit whinnied. Madeline frowned at Leonard and nodded toward the approaching siren. Leonard looked scared. I didn't know whether to be glad to see the police coming or to run for the hills.

I watched the flashing lights as a police car pulled into Happy Trails. And behind them came a little blue car I recognized as Pat Haven's.

Leonard panicked. He bumped past Madeline, almost knocking her down.

But Madeline recovered and waved her arms at the police car. "Here!" she shouted. "We're up here! Hurry!"

Both cars aimed toward us, speeding up the bumpy lane, past the stable, through the pastures.

Leonard thundered over to the fence. "You

kids!" He spat on the ground. "I might have knowed you were behind this."

He stepped on the bottom rung of the fence, as if he meant to climb over. Bandit's ears went back, warning him not to.

Suddenly Mason broke away from Kaylee and ran at Leonard. "No!" he screamed. "No! Don't touch!"

I ran back to them, ducked under the fence, and blocked Mason before he reached Leonard. Then I knelt down and held him tight. "It's okay, Mason. We won't let him touch the horse. It's okay."

The police car tore through the pasture, pulling up a foot from Leonard. A young policeman stepped out of the car and flipped up his sunglasses. "Somebody want to tell me what's going on here?"

"I'll tell you, Officer!" Leonard said. "These little girls were trying to steal my aunt's horse."

"That's a lie!" Kaylee shouted.

"What were you doing?" the policeman asked. He was looking at me. Waiting.

"Well," I said, "we were trying to get Bandit out of the pasture, but—"

"See? She even admits it!" Leonard shouted.

Pat stepped out of her car and ran around to the passenger door. From the backseat a tall man with glasses and a business suit got out. Then I could see who Pat was helping out of the front seat—the old woman we'd seen the first night at Happy Trails.

The woman squinted over at us. "I saw these girls before, from my front porch," she said. "Leonard? What is going on?"

"I caught these girls stealing horses!" Leonard answered.

"We were not stealing your horses!" Kaylee protested. "We were protecting them!"

The policeman turned to Mrs. Pulaski. "Ma'am, are you the owner of Happy Trails?"

"I am," she answered.

He turned to Pat. "And who are you?"

Pat stuck out her hand. "Pat Haven, a friend of the Pulaskis. Mrs. Pulaski phoned me a half hour ago, when this gentleman—" Pat motioned to the guy in glasses, who reminded me of a fit Quarter Horse—"from the American Society for the Prevention of Cruelty to Animals, showed up at her door. We were on our way to the stable when you whizzed past us in your police car. I don't know what's going on, Officer, but I can promise you that those girls wouldn't steal a fly, no offense."

Pat glared at Leonard but still spoke to the policeman. "And if I were you, I wouldn't believe one word Lazy Lenny says."

Quarter Horse Man looked confused. "We had an official complaint against Happy Trails. But I didn't expect police involvement."

"I don't know anything about that," the officer said, scratching his head and gazing around. "Now, which one of you phoned me?"

"That would be me, Officer." Madeline brushed by Leonard, accidentally elbowing him. "I'm the one who called you. Madeline Edison."

"Because someone was stealing a horse?" asked the policeman.

"My, no!" Madeline objected. "Because this . . . this Leonard has been abusing that poor horse over there." She pointed to Bandit.

"Lenny!" Pat frowned at Leonard. "You haven't changed a bit!"

"I want to see my horse," Mrs. Pulaski said, shuffling to the fence, with Pat hanging on to her, as if she thought the woman might break into pieces.

"Are you girls all right?" Pat asked.

"We're okay, Pat," I said. "I'm sure glad to see you, though."

Mrs. Pulaski held on to the fence and let out a gasp. "My poor Buck!" she exclaimed. "What's happened to my buckskin?" She gripped the railing and stuck out her hand toward Bandit.

I watched, amazed, as Bandit's ears flicked. Then he took slow, cautious steps toward the old woman. He walked within a few feet of her and stretched out his neck to sniff her hand.

"Oh, Buck," she said, sobbing. "I am so sorry. I should have looked out for you myself. I should have—"

"You couldn't have done anything more," Pat said, putting her arm around Mrs. Pulaski. Pat turned to Kaylee and me. "She was in the hospital for weeks. The doctor ordered her to stay inside and recover."

Bandit rubbed his head against the woman's hand.

"You love that horse, don't you, Mrs. Pulaski?" I asked, still surprised. I'd misjudged her from the first day.

"I love all my horses." She wheeled on her

nephew so fast that Pat had to keep her from falling. "Leonard, how could you!" she screamed.

"It's those kids, Aunt Ida," Leonard whined.

"We're the ones who have been taking care of Bandit!" Kaylee cried. "We got him to trust us. And it wasn't easy, after what you did to him!" She turned to Mrs. Pulaski. "He was going to get rid of the buckskin. He said so."

Leonard sneered at us. "Well, they ain't your horses, are they? And if I got plans for this here one, you don't got nothing to say about it."

Mrs. Pulaski's round back straightened, and she seemed to grow several inches as her eyes narrowed on Leonard. "Nephew, *you* have nothing to say about it. You're fired!"

Kaylee, Mason, and I broke into applause.

The police officer and Quarter Horse Man from animal protection were so mixed-up that they asked us all to go with them to the Ashland police station and help fill out reports.

At the station, they talked to us together. Then they split us up and asked more questions.

Pat was the first to leave, so she could take Mrs. Pulaski home.

Then Kaylee's parents came for her. They had a lot of questions of their own, but they didn't seem too mad. They were almost out the door when Kaylee came running back. "Thanks, Winnie," she said. "Mrs. Pulaski told me I could come out and see Bandit anytime I wanted. And she offered me a summer job at Happy Trails! I'll have to ask my parents when they've calmed down. But wouldn't that be perfect? I'd see Bandit all the time!"

"That's great, Kaylee!" It was the kind of solution that had God's fingerprints all over it.

I watched Kaylee walk out, with one parent on either side of her. And I felt happy for her, honest-to-goodness happy.

"Winnie!" Dad came racing through the police station, with Lizzy behind him.

Lizzy threw her arms around me. "Winnie, are you okay? Madeline called us and said to meet you at the police station! And Dad's cell phone was scratchy. We knew it wasn't an accident, but—"

"Winnie, are you all right? I was so worried about you!" Dad hugged me so hard I coughed.

"I'm sorry, Dad. I shouldn't have left without talking to you."

"Well, it's about time!" Madeline shouted across the police station. She and Mason came out of the deputy's office and joined Lizzy, Dad, and me. "We need to have a little talk, Jack," Madeline continued. "I think you've been a little leaf-blocked lately where Winnie's concerned."

Dad's forehead wrinkled, like when he's stuck on an invention. "I've been what-blocked?"

Madeline took his elbow and led him to the nearest chair. "Winnie," she called back, "don't worry about Leonard. I made them promise that he would never be allowed near another horse again." She waved a piece of paper at me. "I got it in writing!"

"Leonard?" Dad asked, looking dazed. "Who's Leonard?"

"Way to go, Madeline!" I shouted.

Madeline sat Dad down on a bench in the corner, while she stood in front of him, her mouth moving as fast as a gallop. I figured she was filling him in on everything, and then some.

Lizzy scratched her head. "You and Madeline? I want the whole story, Winnie. But first, promise me that you're all right. When we had to leave for Columbus without you, I felt terrible."

Columbus! The state science fair. "Lizzy, how did it go in Columbus? Did you win?" I looked behind her, as if she might have hidden her trophy there.

She shook her head. "M didn't win either. But he had great conversations with just about every girl in the contest, thanks to that conversation ball." She smiled weakly, but I could see through it. "I didn't even get an honorable mention."

I felt like I was going to cry. "Lizzy, I'm really sorry."

She shrugged. "Dad was pretty disappointed. He tried hard not to show it. But he's not much of an actor."

I laughed. I knew exactly what she meant. "I should have been there for you, Lizzy."

"You had to save that horse, Winnie. You would have been there if you could have."

But I knew better. Columbus had been the last place I'd wanted to be. "Lizzy, I didn't want to go there and watch you and Dad. I've been kind of mixed-up. When you won at the science fair, I wanted to be happy for you. But I kept seeing how close you and Dad were, how happy you guys were. And it felt horrible. I couldn't even be happy for you, Lizzy."

"Winnie, that's what I've been struggling with too! I mean, I did want you to win. I really did. But I hated every second in that barn." She grinned. "And I wanted to spend that much time with Dad too. I kept fighting the feeling that it was so unfair."

I laughed out loud. Unfair. It was unfair, but I sure hadn't seen it that way. Leaf-blocked.

"You know," I said, "I don't think I cared that much about the science fair. I just wanted Dad to be proud of me. He's always proud of you. What parent wouldn't be proud of a popular, kind, A+ student, Lizzy?"

"Me? Winnie, are you kidding? Even in Columbus, Dad bragged to perfect strangers about Winnie the Horse Gentler."

"He did?" I glanced at Dad. Madeline was still talking, using her hands. Behind her, Mason waved his arms, as if mimicking his mom.

Officer Stufflebean, the young policeman, with sunglasses now tucked in his front pocket, came over. "Winnie, is this your twin?"

Lizzy and I laughed. He wasn't the first one to make that mistake.

Lizzy grinned at him. "Well, we were the same age yesterday."

"Officer Stufflebean," I said, "I'd like you to meet my amazing sister, Lizzy, the great inventor."

I rode home with Dad and Lizzy in the cattle truck. Madeline and Mason followed us in the van.

As soon as we turned onto our street, I knew something was up. I leaned out the window and smelled horse. Not just my horses. Lots of horses.

As we got closer, I spotted Hawk sitting bareback on Towaco. Sal was holding Amigo on a long lead, as the Miniature Falabella grazed on our unmown grass. I saw Grant and Eager Star. Catman had my beautiful Nickers, and M was leading Buddy. Barker came walking out of the barn with Annie Goat.

"What's going on?" I asked as Dad turned off the engine.

187

"You didn't think we'd forget your birthday party, did you, Winnie?" Dad answered. "I couldn't sleep last night, honey. You deserve a real birthday. This morning I called Hawk and worked out everything." He leaned over and hugged me. "Happy birthday, Winnie Willis."

"Happy birthday, Winnie!" Lizzy exclaimed. She hugged both of us, then jumped down from the truck. "You're late to your own party."

"Man, where have you been?" Sal shouted.

"Long story, Sal," I answered, hopping down after Lizzy.

"The horses started partying without you." Sal pointed to Amigo, enjoying the grass feast.

"I'll get the cake!" Lizzy said.

"Cake?" I asked, trying to take it all in.

"I hid it in the pots-and-pans cupboard. Didn't think you'd go there."

"You're right about that," I agreed.

"Buddy!" Mason jogged over to his filly and hugged her, while M held the lead. M winked at me. Then he and Mason high-fived each other.

It was great to see Mason so happy. I could feel it. Share it. *"When others are happy, be happy with them."* It was a good thing, sharing joy. I

188

was going to try to remember that. I'd wasted too much joy being leaf-blocked by envy.

"Happy birthday, Winnie." Hawk grinned at me from Towaco's back. She must have had to call everybody herself to pull off the party.

"Thanks, Hawk."

"Happy birthday, Winnie," Grant said, leading Eager Star up so I could pat him. "Summer can't make it."

"Too bad," I said, trying not to smile. But Grant smiled back. "Scar acting up on her?" I asked.

"More like Columbus embarrassment, I think," Grant said.

"Huh?"

"Didn't your sister tell you?" Hawk asked. "Summer got disqualified at the state science fair."

"You're kidding!" Now I really wished I'd gone to Columbus.

"She got busted!" Sal explained. "Turns out her 'original' finger-combs were 'made in Japan.'"

Note to self: Maybe some things aren't so unfair, if you wait long enough.

Catman waved, and Nickers nickered. I went to my horse and threw my arms around her neck. With Catman holding her leadrope, I swung up bareback.

"Cool day of your birth," Catman said.

"Thanks, Catman."

From Nickers' back, I scanned our lawn, still filled with junk. But it was also filled with horses and people who cared enough about me to come to my birthday party. The sun was setting, throwing shadows across the lawn and bringing a chilly breeze, and I prayed that my mind would snap a picture of this moment.

Lizzy and Dad came out of the house with a big cake for us and cake-shaped, oatmeal-and-molasses treats for the horses. Next year I'd throw both of them birthday parties.

Out in the road came the *clip-clop* of a horse's hooves. Kaylee was riding toward us on Buckskin Bandit, with Pat Haven walking beside her.

"Winnie, look!" Kaylee cried. "Pat told Mrs. Pulaski about your party, and she wanted me to bring Bandit."

I waved. Bandit looked happy and calm, at home with his new herd.

As I gazed across the lawn—from one person, one horse, to another—I felt as if God were whispering in my ear: *It's unfair, isn't it, Winnie?*

Unfair. With the leaf down, I could see now. I hadn't done anything to deserve a herd like this—friends, family, horses. A God who died for me so I could have a life like this and a God who whispers in my ear.

You're right, God. It is unfair. Thanks.

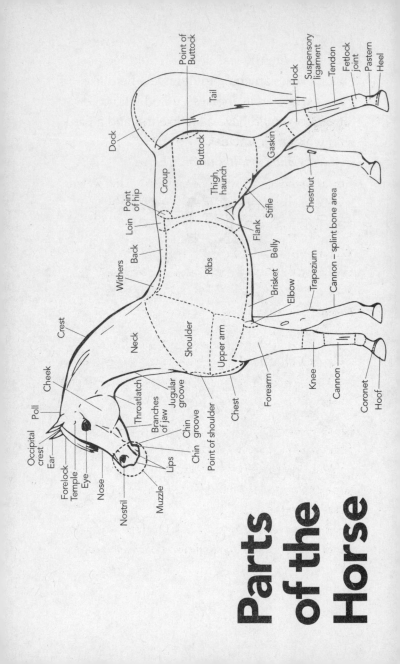

Parts
of the
Horse

Point of Buttock
Hock
Suspensory ligament
Tendon
Fetlock joint
Pastern
Heel
Tail
Dock
Buttock
Gaskin
Croup
Thigh, haunch
Stifle
Chestnut
Cannon – splint bone area
Point of hip
Loin
Flank
Withers
Back
Ribs
Belly
Trapezium
Crest
Neck
Shoulder
Brisket
Elbow
Upper arm
Cannon
Cheek
Poll
Throatlatch
Jugular groove
Forearm
Knee
Branches of jaw
Chin groove
Chest
Coronet
Hoof
Occipital crest
Ear
Chin
Point of shoulder
Forelock
Temple
Eye
Nose
Lips
Nostril
Muzzle

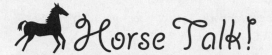# Horse Talk!

Horses communicate with one another . . . and with us, if we learn to read their cues. Here are some of the main ways a horse talks:

Whinny—A loud, long horse call that can be heard from a half mile away. Horses often whinny back and forth.
Possible translations: Is that you over there? Hello! I'm over here! See me? I heard you! What's going on?

Neigh—To most horse people, a neigh is the same as a whinny. Some people call any vocalization from a horse a neigh.

Nicker—The friendliest horse greeting in the world. A nicker is a low sound made in the throat, sometimes rumbling. Horses use it as a warm greeting for another horse or a trusted person. A horse owner might hear a nicker at feeding time.
Possible translations: Welcome back! Good to see you. I missed you. Hey there! Come on over. Got anything good to eat?

Snort—This sounds like your snort, only much louder and more fluttering. It's a hard exhale, with the air being forced out through the nostrils.
Possible translations: Look out! Something's wrong out there! Yikes! What's that?

Blow—Usually one huge exhale, like a snort, but in a large burst of wind.
Possible translations: What's going on? Things aren't so bad. Such is life.

Squeal—This high-pitched cry that sounds a bit like a scream can be heard a hundred yards away.
Possible translations: Don't you dare! Stop it! I'm warning you! I've had it—I mean it! That hurts!

Grunts, groans, sighs, sniffs—Horses make a variety of sounds. Some grunts and groans mean nothing more than boredom. Others are natural outgrowths of exercise.

*****

Horses also communicate without making a sound. You'll need to observe each horse and tune in to the individual translations, but here are some possible versions of nonverbal horse talk:

EARS
Flat back ears—When a horse pins back its ears, pay attention and beware! If the ears go back slightly, the

horse may just be irritated. The closer the ears are pressed back to the skull, the angrier the horse.

Possible translations: I don't like that buzzing fly. You're making me mad! I'm warning you! You try that, and I'll make you wish you hadn't!

Pricked forward, stiff ears—Ears stiffly forward usually mean a horse is on the alert. Something ahead has captured its attention.

Possible translations: What's that? Did you hear that? I want to know what that is! Forward ears may also say, *I'm cool and proud of it!*

Relaxed, loosely forward ears—When a horse is content, listening to sounds all around, ears relax, tilting loosely forward.

Possible translations: It's a fine day, not too bad at all. Nothin' new out here.

Uneven ears—When a horse swivels one ear up and one ear back, it's just paying attention to the surroundings.

Possible translations: Sigh. So, anything interesting going on yet?

Stiff, twitching ears—If a horse twitches stiff ears, flicking them fast (in combination with overall body tension), be on guard! This horse may be terrified and ready to bolt.

Possible translations: Yikes! I'm outta here! Run for the hills!

Airplane ears—Ears lopped to the sides usually means the horse is bored or tired.
Possible translations: Nothing ever happens around here. So, what's next already? Bor-ing.

Droopy ears—When a horse's ears sag and droop to the sides, it may just be sleepy, or it might be in pain.
Possible translations: Yawn . . . I am so sleepy. I could sure use some shut-eye. I don't feel so good. It really hurts.

TAIL

Tail switches hard and fast—An intensely angry horse will switch its tail hard enough to hurt anyone foolhardy enough to stand within striking distance. The tail flies side to side and maybe up and down as well.
Possible translations: I've had it, I tell you! Enough is enough! Stand back and get out of my way!

Tail held high—A horse who holds its tail high may be proud to be a horse!
Possible translations: Get a load of me! Hey! Look how gorgeous I am! I'm so amazing that I just may hightail it out of here!

Clamped-down tail—Fear can make a horse clamp its tail to its rump.
Possible translations: I don't like this; it's scary. What are they going to do to me? Can't somebody help me?

Pointed tail swat—One sharp, well-aimed swat of the tail could mean something hurts there.

Possible translations: Ouch! That hurts! Got that pesky fly.

OTHER SIGNALS

Pay attention to other body language. Stamping a hoof may mean impatience or eagerness to get going. A rear hoof raised slightly off the ground might be a sign of irritation. The same hoof raised, but relaxed, may signal sleepiness. When a horse is angry, the muscles tense, back stiffens, and the eyes flash, showing extra white of the eyeballs. One anxious horse may balk, standing stone still and stiff legged. Another horse just as anxious may dance sideways or paw the ground. A horse in pain might swing its head backward toward the pain, toss its head, shiver, or try to rub or nibble the sore spot. Sick horses tend to lower their heads and look dull, listless, and unresponsive.

As you attempt to communicate with your horse and understand what he or she is saying, remember that different horses may use the same sound or signal, but mean different things. One horse may flatten her ears in anger, while another horse lays back his ears to listen to a rider. Each horse has his or her own language, and it's up to you to understand.

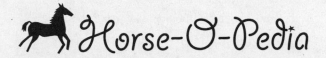

Horse-O-Pedia

Advance and Retreat—A patient method of horse gentling that allows the horse to choose to hook up with a trainer. The horse can take steps toward the trainer and be rewarded with "friendly" body language.

Akhal Teke—A small, compact horse with an elegant head. The Akhal Teke, also known as Turkmen, is fast, strong, and reliable—a great, all-around riding horse.

American Saddlebred (or American Saddle Horse)—A showy breed of horse with five gaits (walk, trot, canter, and two extras). They are usually high-spirited, often high-strung; mainly seen in horse shows.

Andalusian—A breed of horse originating in Spain, strong and striking in appearance. They have been used in dressage, as parade horses, in the bullring, and even for herding cattle.

Appaloosa—Horse with mottled skin and a pattern of spots, such as a solid white or brown with oblong, dark spots behind the withers. They're usually good all-around horses.

Arabian—Believed to be the oldest breed or one of the oldest. Arabians are thought by many to be the most beautiful of all horses. They are characterized by a small head, large eyes, refined build, silky mane and tail, and often high spirits.

Barb—North African desert horse.

Bay—A horse with a mahogany or deep brown to reddish-brown color and a black mane and tail.

Blind-age—Without revealing age.

Buck—To thrust out the back legs, kicking off the ground.

Buckskin—Tan or grayish-yellow-colored horse with black mane and tail.

Caballero—A Spanish or Latin horseman. A cowboy.

Camargue—A tough, surefooted, but high-stepping and beautiful horse native to southern France. Camargues have inspired artists and poets down through the centuries.

Cannon—The bone in a horse's leg that runs from the knee to the fetlock.

Canter—A rolling-gait with a three time pace slower than a gallop. The rhythm falls with the right hind foot, then the left hind and right fore simultaneously, then the left fore followed by a period of suspension when all feet are off the ground.

Cattle-pony stop—Sudden, sliding stop with drastically bent haunches and rear legs; the type of stop a cutting, or cowboy, horse might make to round up cattle.

Chestnut—A horse with a coat colored golden yellow to dark brown, sometimes the color of bays, but with same-color mane and tail.

Cloverleaf—The three-cornered racing pattern followed in many barrel races; so named because the circles around each barrel resemble the three petals on a clover leaf.

Clydesdale—A very large and heavy draft breed. Clydesdales have been used for many kinds of work, from towing barges along canals, to plowing fields, to hauling heavy loads in wagons.

Colic—A digestive disorder in horses, accompanied by severe abdominal pain.

Colostrum—First milk. The first milk that comes from a mare contains the antibodies the foal needs to prevent disease.

Conformation—The overall structure of a horse; the way his parts fit together. Good conformation in a horse means that horse is solidly built, with straight legs and well-proportioned features.

Crop—A small whip sometimes used by riders.

Cross-ties—Two straps coming from opposite walls of the stallway. They hook onto a horse's halter for easier grooming.

Curb—A single-bar bit with a curve in the middle and shanks and a curb chain to provide leverage in a horse's mouth.

Dapple—A color effect that looks splotchy. A dapple-gray horse will be light gray, covered with rings of darker gray.

D ring—The D-shaped, metal ring on the side of a horse's halter.

Dun—A yellowish or gold color overall on the body of a horse, with black or dark brown points as a stripe on the back, legs, and withers.

Dutch Friesian—A stocky, large European breed of horses who have characteristically bushy manes.

English Riding—The style of riding English or Eastern or Saddle Seat, on a flat saddle that's lighter and leaner than a Western saddle. English riding is seen in three-gaited and five-gaited Saddle Horse classes in horse shows. In competition, the rider posts at the trot and wears a formal riding habit.

Falabella—The smallest horse in the world, a miniature horse rather than a pony, standing less than 34 inches, usually 20–32 inches. Falabellas were first seen in herds of Mapuche Indians of Argentina and first bred by the Falabella family.

Founder—A condition, also known as laminitis, in which the hoof becomes deformed due to poor blood circulation. Major causes are getting too much of spring's first grass, overeating, drinking cold water immediately after exercise, excessive stress, or other ailments.

Frog—The soft, V-shaped section on the underside of a horse's hoof.

Gait—Set manner in which a horse moves. Horses have four natural gaits: the walk, the trot or jog, the canter or lope, and the gallop. Other gaits have been learned or are characteristic to certain breeds: pace, amble, slow gait, rack, running walk, etc.

Galvayne's Groove—The groove on the surface of a horse's upper incisor. The length of the Galvayne's groove is a good way to determine a horse's age.

Gelding—An altered male horse.

Hackamore—A bridle with no bit, often used for training Western horses. Also known as a bitless bridle.

Hackney—A high-stepping harness horse driven in

show rings. Hackneys used to pull carriages in everyday life.

Halter—Basic device of straps or rope fitting around a horse's head and behind the ears. Halters are used to lead or tie up a horse.

Hand or **Hands high**—The unit of measure to describe a horse's height. A hand equals four inches (10 cm). Horses are said to be a certain number of "hands high."

Hay net—A net or open bag that can be filled with hay and hung in a stall. Hay nets provide an alternate method of feeding hay to horses.

Headshy—Touchy around the head. Horses that are headshy may jerk their heads away when someone attempts to stroke their heads or to bridle them.

Heaves—A disease that makes it hard for the horse to breathe. Heaves in horses is similar to asthma in humans.

Hippotherapy—A specialty area of therapeutic horse riding that has been used to help patients with neurological disorders, movement dysfunctions, and other disabilities. Hippotherapy is a medical treatment given by a specially trained physical therapist.

Horse Therapy—A form of treatment where the patient is encouraged to form a partnership with the therapy horse.

Hunter—A horse used primarily for hunt riding. Hunter is a type, not a distinct breed. Many hunters are bred in Ireland, Britain, and the U.S.

Imprinting—A learning process, generally referring to gentling a newborn foal, in which a behavior pattern is established and the foal bonds with a human. The foal is touched and handled in much the same way a mare would nuzzle her foal.

Join up—A method of horse gentling, made popular by the famous trainer Monty Roberts, who applied principles he observed in herd behavior. Joining up is the moment when a horse chooses to step toward the trainer and become part of the trainer's herd.

Leadrope—A rope with a hook on one end to attach to a horse's halter for leading or tying the horse.

Leads—The act of a horse galloping in such a way as to balance his body, leading with one side or the other. In a *right lead*, the right foreleg leaves the ground last and seems to reach out farther. In a *left lead*, the horse reaches out farther with the left foreleg, usually when galloping counterclockwise.

Lipizzaner—Strong, stately horse used in the famous Spanish Riding School of Vienna. Lipizzaners are born black and turn gray or white.

Lunge line (longe line)—A very long lead line or rope, used for exercising a horse from the ground. A hook at one end of the line is attached to the horse's halter, and the horse is encouraged to move in a circle around the handler.

Lusitano—Large, agile, noble breed of horse from Portugal. They're known as the mounts of bullfighters.

Manipur—A pony bred in Manipur, India. Descended from the wild Mongolian horse, the Manipur was the original polo pony.

Mare—Female horse.

Maremmano—A classical Greek warhorse descended from sixteenth-century Spain. It was the preferred mount of the Italian cowboy.

Martingale—A strap run from the girth, between a horse's forelegs, and up to the reins or noseband of the bridle. The martingale restricts a horse's head movements.

Miniature or **Mini**—A unique breed of horse that is an elegant, scaled-down version of the large-size horse. Miniature horses can't be taller than 34 inches.

Morgan—A compact, solidly built breed of horse with muscular shoulders. Morgans are usually reliable, trustworthy horses.

Mustang—Originally, a small, hardy Spanish horse turned loose in the wilds. Mustangs still run wild in protected parts of the U.S. They are suspicious of humans, tough, hard to train, but quick and able horses.

Paddock—Fenced area near a stable or barn; smaller than a pasture. It's often used for training and working horses.

Paint—A spotted horse with Quarter Horse or Thoroughbred bloodlines. The American Paint Horse Association registers only those horses with Paint, Quarter Horse, or Thoroughbred registration papers.

Palomino—Cream-colored or golden horse with a silver or white mane and tail.

Palouse—Native American people who inhabited the Washington–Oregon area. They were highly skilled in horse training and are credited with developing the Appaloosas.

Percheron—A heavy, hardy breed of horse with a good disposition. Percherons have been used as elegant draft horses, pulling royal coaches. They've also been good workhorses on farms. Thousands of Percherons from America served as warhorses during World War I.

Peruvian Paso—A smooth and steady horse with a weird gait that's kind of like swimming. *Paso* means "step"; the Peruvian Paso can step out at 16 MPH without giving the rider a bumpy ride.

Pinto—Spotted horse, brown and white or black and white. Refers only to color. The Pinto Horse Association registers any spotted horse or pony.

Poll—The highest part of a horse's head, right between the ears.

Post—A riding technique in English horsemanship. The rider posts to a rising trot, lifting slightly out of the saddle and back down, in coordination with the horse's bounciest gait, the trot.

Presentation—The way the foal comes out at birth. Normal presentation is for a foal to have two front hooves appear, followed by the nose between the legs.

Przewalski—Perhaps the oldest breed of primitive horse. Also known as the Mongolian Wild Horse, the Przewalski Horse looks primitive, with a large head and a short, broad body.

Quarter Horse—A muscular "cowboy" horse reminiscent of the Old West. The Quarter Horse got its name from the fact that it can outrun other horses over the quarter mile. Quarter Horses are usually easygoing and good-natured.

Quirt—A short-handled rawhide whip sometimes used by riders.

Rear—To suddenly lift both front legs into the air and stand only on the back legs.

Roan—The color of a horse when white hairs mix with the basic coat of black, brown, chestnut, or gray.

Round pen—Small circular pen, used for horse gentling, using such methods as joining up and advance and retreat.

Saddle horn—The raised front piece, or horn, of the Western saddle.

Snaffle—A single bar bit, often jointed, or "broken" in the middle, with no shank. Snaffle bits are generally considered less punishing than curbed bits.

Sorrel—Used to describe a horse that's reddish (usually reddish-brown) in color.

Spur—A short metal spike or spiked wheel that straps to the heel of a rider's boots. Spurs are used to urge the horse on faster.

Stallion—An unaltered male horse.

Standardbred—A breed of horse heavier than the Thoroughbred, but similar in type. Standardbreds have a calm temperament and are used in harness racing.

Stifle—The joint between the thigh and the gaskin—the hip joint.

Surcingle—A type of cinch used to hold a saddle, blanket, or a pack to a horse. The surcingle looks like a wide belt.

Tack—Horse equipment (saddles, bridles, halters, etc.).

Tarpan—A hardy, native breed of pony that survived on the tough terrain of Russia, the Carpathian Mountains, and the Ukraine. The original Tarpan is extinct, but a related breed exists in Poland.

Tennessee Walker—A gaited horse, with a running walk—half walk and half trot. Tennessee Walking Horses are generally steady and reliable, very comfortable to ride.

Thoroughbred—The fastest breed of horse in the world, they are used as racing horses. Thoroughbreds are often high-strung.

Three-gaited—A type of American Saddle Horse that performs in classes where only the walk, trot, and canter are called for.

Thrush—An infection in the V-shaped frog of a horse's foot. Thrush can be caused by a horse's standing in a dirty stall or wet pasture.

Tie short—Tying the rope with little or no slack to prevent movement from the horse.

Trakehner—Strong, dependable, agile horse that can do it all—show, dressage, jump, harness.

Trotter—Generally a horse, such as a Standardbred or Hackney, that is bred to run in harness, strictly at a trot.

Turnout time—Time a horse spends outside a barn or stable, "turned out" to exercise or roam in a pasture.

Twitch—A device some horsemen use to make a horse go where it doesn't want to go. A rope noose loops around the upper lip. The loop is attached to what looks like a bat, and the bat is twisted, tightening the noose around the horse's muzzle until he gives in.

Waxing—The formation of thick drops of first milk that begin leaking from a mare's udders. It may look like honey or wax.

Welsh Cob—A breed of pony brought to the U.S. from the United Kingdom. Welsh Cobs are great all-around ponies.

Western Riding—The style of riding as cowboys of the Old West rode, as ranchers have ridden, with a traditional Western saddle, heavy, deep-seated, with a raised saddle horn. Trail riding and pleasure riding are generally Western; more relaxed than English riding.

Wind sucking—The bad, and often dangerous, habit of some stabled horses to chew on fence or stall wood and suck in air.

 **Author Talk**

Dandi Daley Mackall grew up riding horses, taking her first solo bareback ride when she was three. Her best friends were Sugar, a Pinto; Misty, probably a Morgan; and Towaco, an Appaloosa; along with Ash Bill, a Quarter Horse; Rocket, a buckskin; Angel, the colt; Butch, anybody's guess; Lancer and Cindy, American Saddlebreds; and Moby, a white Quarter Horse. Dandi and husband, Joe; daughters, Jen and Katy; and son, Dan (when forced) enjoy riding Cheyenne, their Paint. Dandi has written books for all ages, including Little Blessings books, Degrees of Guilt: *Kyra's Story*, Degrees of Betrayal: *Sierra's Story, Love Rules*, and *Maggie's Story*. Her books (about 400 titles) have sold more than 4 million copies. She writes and rides from rural Ohio.

Visit Dandi at www.dandibooks.com.

S·T·A·R·L·I·G·H·T

Animal Rescue

More than just animals need rescuing in this new series. Starlight Animal Rescue is where problem horses are trained and loved, where abandoned dogs become heroes, where stray cats become loyal companions. And where people with nowhere to fit in find a place to belong.

Entire series available now!

#1 *Runaway*

#2 *Mad Dog*

#3 *Wild Cat*

#4 *Dark Horse*

Read all four to discover how a group of teens cope with life and disappointment.

Winnie
The Horse Gentler

1. WILD THING
2. EAGER STAR
3. BOLD BEAUTY
4. MIDNIGHT MYSTERY
5. UNHAPPY APPY
6. GIFT HORSE
7. FRIENDLY FOAL
8. BUCKSKIN BANDIT

COLLECT ALL EIGHT BOOKS!

Can't get enough of Winnie? Visit her Web site to read more about Winnie and her friends plus all about their horses.

IT'S ALL ON WINNIETHEHORSEGENTLER.COM

There are so many fun and cool things to do on Winnie's Web site; here are just a few:

⭐ PAT'S PETS

Post your favorite photo of your pet and tell us a fun story about them

⭐ ASK WINNIE

Here's your chance to ask Winnie questions about your horse

✦ MANE ATTRACTION

Meet Dandi and her horse, Cheyenne!

⭐ THE BARNYARD

Here's your chance to share your thoughts with others

✦ AND MUCH MORE!